THE SISTERS GRIMM

3

THE S

GRI

10th Anniversary Edition

SISTERS GRIMM

THE PROBLEM CHILD

MICHAEL BUCKLEY

Pictures by PETER FERGUSON

AMULET BOOKS   NEW YORK

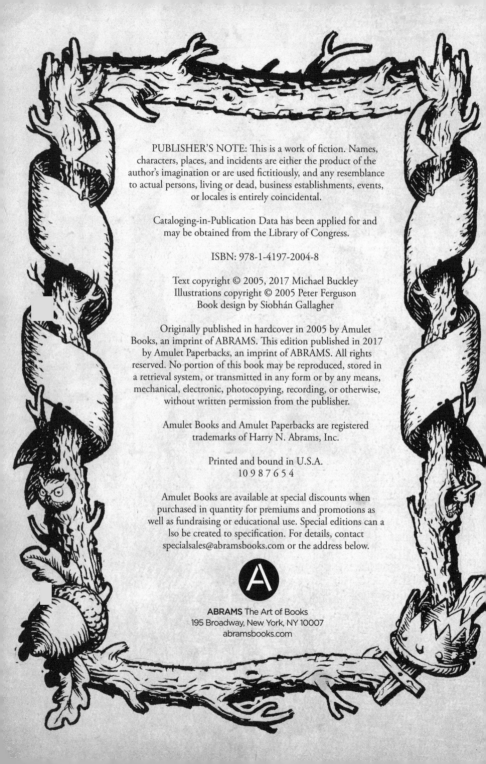

Cataloging-in-Publication Data has been applied for and may be obtained from the Library of Congress.

ISBN: 978-1-4197-2004-8

Text copyright © 2005, 2017 Michael Buckley
Illustrations copyright © 2005 Peter Ferguson
Book design by Siobhán Gallagher

Printed and bound in U.S.A.
10 9 8 7 6 5 4

Amulet Books are available at special discounts when purchased in quantity for premiums and promotions as well as fundraising or educational use. Special editions can a lso be created to specification. For details, contact specialsales@abramsbooks.com or the address below.

ABRAMS The Art of Books
195 Broadway, New York, NY 10007
abramsbooks.com

For the kids,
Dominic, Kierra, Kiah, Tulia,
Siena, and Dan-Dan

*H*e descended from the clouds like an angel, enveloped in a ray of light so brilliant that Sabrina and Daphne had to shield their eyes. When he landed nimbly on the ground, the light dimmed just enough so that they could see his face. Aside from his smile, the man he had been just moments before was gone, his flesh replaced by shimmering crystal, his eyes by blazing fires, like two small suns shining down. He stepped toward them with extended arms, and they stumbled back in fear. His smile quickly turned to a frown.

"What are you doing?" Sabrina demanded.

"I'm granting myself a wish," he answered. "I'm giving myself the power to make the people I love happy. I've been miserable. Happy is better. You can be happy, too. Wish for something, Sabrina. Anything. I can make it happen."

"But look at the cost!" Granny Relda said as she hovered over Mayor Charming's rapidly aging body. His beloved Snow White lay next to him, reaching with bony, arthritic hands to touch his wrinkled face. Everywhere Sabrina looked, Everafters lay struggling against the sudden onrush of old age. Many were in the final throes of death.

"Don't cry for them," the glittering being said to the old woman. "The Everafters have had their day in the sun, and it was a long, long day. With their power I can re-create this world as a paradise where 'happily ever after' isn't just for a bunch of bedtime stories come to life. It's time for all our dreams to come true!"

1

Five Days Earlier

SABRINA OPENED HER EYES AND SAW A MONSTER hunched over her. It was nearly fifteen feet tall, with scaly skin, two black leathery wings, and a massive serpentine tail that lashed back and forth. Its feet and hands were enormous, nearly as big as its body, and its head, at the end of a long, snakelike neck, was nothing but teeth—thousands of jagged fangs, gnashing in her face. A drop of saliva dripped from the creature's mouth and landed on her forehead. It was as hot as molten lava. "JABBERWOCKY!" the monster roared.

Too afraid to move, Sabrina closed her eyes and did the only thing she could. She prayed. *Please! Please! Please! Let this be a bad dream!*

After a few moments she slowly lifted one eyelid. Unfortunately, the monster was still there.

"Fudge," Sabrina whispered.

"Well, *good morning*!" a boy's voice called from somewhere in the room.

Sabrina knew its owner. "Puck?"

"Did we wake you? So sorry!"

"Could you get this thing off of me?" asked Sabrina.

"It's gonna cost you."

"What?"

"I figure if I'm going to have to save your butt every time you get into trouble, I might as well be paid for it. The going rate for this kind of job is seven million dollars," Puck said.

"Where am I going to get seven million dollars? I'm eleven years old!"

"And I want all your desserts for the next six months," Puck added.

The monster roared in Sabrina's face. A long, purple tongue darted out of the beast's mouth and roughly licked her face.

"Fine!" Sabrina cried.

Puck leaped into the air, flipping like an Olympic gymnast, and clung to a dusty light fixture hanging from the ceiling above. Gathering momentum, he swung down feet-first into the monster's horrible face. The creature stumbled back and roared. Using its face as a springboard, the nimble boy flipped again and landed on his feet with his hands on his hips. He turned to Sabrina and winked, then pulled her to her feet. "Did you see that landing, Grimm? I want to make sure you get your money's worth."

Sabrina scowled. "How long was I unconscious?" she asked. Her head was still pounding from the smack the beast had given her when she stepped through the portal.

"Long enough for me to get old big-and-ugly here pretty angry," Puck said as the brute recovered and charged at the children at an impossible speed.

Two enormous wings popped out of Puck's back and flapped wildly. Before Sabrina knew it, he had snatched the back of her coat and was pulling her into the air, narrowly avoiding the beast's attack. The Jabberwocky crashed through the wall behind them.

"I've got the big one," Puck said as he set Sabrina back down on the floor. "You take the little one."

Sabrina followed his gaze. In the far corner of the room was a small child wearing a long red cloak that hung to her ankles. She sat on a dirty hospital cot next to the unconscious bodies of two adults, Henry and Veronica Grimm—Sabrina's parents!

How Sabrina had gotten into this particular situation was a long, and almost unbelievable, story. It had started a year and a half ago, when her mother and father mysteriously disappeared. The only clue the police found was a bloodred handprint pressed onto the dashboard of their abandoned car. With nothing else to go on and no next-of-kin to step in as guardians, Sabrina and her little sister, Daphne, were forced into foster care, where things went from bad to worse. The girls were bounced from one foster home to the next, each filled with certifiable lunatics who used the girls as maids, gardeners, and, once, a couple of amateur roofers. By the time their long-lost grandmother finally tracked them down, Sabrina didn't think she could ever trust anyone again. Granny Relda didn't make it easy, either. They hadn't been in the old woman's house ten minutes before she started telling incredible stories about the girls being the last living descendants of Jacob and Wilhelm Grimm, also known as the Brothers Grimm. Jacob and Wilhelm's book of fairy tales, she claimed, wasn't a collection of bedtime stories but the case files of their detective work investigating unusual crimes. Granny Relda claimed that their new hometown, Ferryport Landing, was filled to the brim with characters straight from fairy tales, who now called themselves "Everafters" and lived side by side with the normal inhabitants of the town, albeit in magical disguises to hide their true identities.

To Sabrina, Granny's stories sounded like the silly ravings of a woman who might have forgotten to get her prescriptions filled, but there was a dark side to her story as well. These Everafters didn't just live in the town—they were trapped there. Jacob and Wilhelm had put a spell on the town to prevent the Everafters from leaving and waging war on humans. The spell could be broken only when the last member of the Grimm family died or abandoned the town. Sabrina warned her sister that the old woman's stories were nonsense, but when Relda was kidnapped by a two-hundred-foot-tall giant, Sabrina could no longer deny the truth. Luckily, the girls found a way to rescue their grandmother—and ever since, they had found themselves knee-deep in the family responsibility of being fairy-tale detectives, solving the town's weirdest crimes, and going head-to-head with some of its most dangerous residents.

As they solved one mystery after another, the girls started to uncover a disturbing pattern. Every bad guy they faced was a member of a shadowy group known as the Scarlet Hand, whose mark was a bloodred handprint just like the one the police had found in Sabrina and Daphne's parents' car! Sabrina knew one day she would come face-to-face with the group's leader and her parents' kidnapper, and now, as she stared at the strange little girl in the red cloak, she was shocked. She'd never thought the person behind all her misery would be a child.

Sabrina clenched her fists, ready to fight her parents' captor, only to have a pain shoot through her left arm that nearly knocked her to the floor. It was broken. She shook off the agony and fixed her eyes once more on the child.

The little girl was no older than Daphne, but her face was that of a twisted, rage-filled adult, barely containing the insanity behind her eyes. Sabrina had seen a man with that expression on the news once. The police had arrested him for strangling five people.

"Get away from my parents," Sabrina demanded as she grabbed the little girl's cloak in her good hand.

"This is my mommy and daddy," the little girl shrieked as she jerked away. "I have a baby brother and a kitty, too. When I get my grandma and my puppy, then we can all be a family and play house."

The girl raised her hand. It was covered in what Sabrina hoped was red paint. She turned and pressed it against the wall, leaving an all-too-familiar scarlet print. There were more just like it on the walls, floors, ceilings, and windows.

"I don't need a sister," the girl continued. "But you can stay and play with my kitty." She pointed at the monster, which was swatting at Puck with its enormous clawed hands. The fairy boy leaped out of the way, barely dodging the "kitty's" lightning-fast strikes. It whipped its tail at Puck, missed, then sent a filing cabinet careening across the room. The drawers swung open, and hundreds of yellowing documents spilled out.

"C'mon, ugly, you can do better than that!" Puck crowed just before the Jabberwocky caught him with its long tail and sent him flailing across the room. He crashed against a wall and tumbled to the floor but quickly sprang to his feet and snatched up the little wooden sword he kept in his belt. With a thrust he bonked the beast on the snout.

Sabrina turned back to the little girl.

"Who are you?" she asked.

"You don't want to play, do you?" the girl said as a frown cracked her face. She reached into her pocket and removed a small silver ring, slipped it onto her finger, and held out her hand. A crimson light engulfed her and Sabrina's sleeping parents. "Kitty, we need to find a new playhouse. Burn this one down."

The monster opened its enormous mouth, and a burst of flame shot out. The folding blinds on the dingy windows ignited, and flames crept up the walls, turning the weathered wallpaper to ash. The beast blasted another wall and then another, sending sparks and cinders in all directions. Within seconds the entire room was on fire.

"Who are you?" Sabrina screamed.

"Tell my grandma and my puppy that I'll see them soon. Then we can play," the demented child said in a singsong voice. The world seemed to stretch, as if someone were pulling on the corners of Sabrina's vision, and, in a blink, the strange child vanished into thin air, taking Sabrina's parents with her.

"*No!*" Sabrina cried, rushing to the empty bed as flames ate at the walls around her. It wasn't long before everything was devoured by fire and smoke. A terrible groan came from above, and a huge section of the ceiling collapsed right on top of the beast. The two children staggered back from the pile of smoldering debris. Puck grabbed Sabrina and dragged her toward an exit as parts of the ceiling rained down around them.

"I think this party is over," he said.

"Wait!" Sabrina shouted. "There could be a clue here to where she took my parents."

"Any clue is kindling now," Puck replied, pulling her down a hallway.

"We can't go!"

"If you get killed, the old lady will never let me hear the end of it."

They passed by open rooms with doors torn off their hinges. Each was full of hospital beds, rusty metal carts, and more sheets of yellowing paper scattered on the floor. In every room she saw more of the horrible red handprints.

What is this place? Sabrina wondered.

The children rushed on through the choking black smoke until they found a door that led outside. Puck forced it open, and a blast of icy wind nearly knocked them down. Snow blew into their faces, temporarily blinding them.

"We're in the mountains, I think!" he shouted.

"Can you fly us out of here?" Sabrina asked.

"The wind is too strong," Puck said, wrapping his arm around her and guiding her through the snowdrifts.

They'd barely taken a dozen steps when the wall surrounding

the building exploded behind them, sending brick and mortar flying in every direction. Through the gaping hole stepped the massive, scaly foot of the Jabberwocky. Its head followed, whipping around on its long neck as its fiery eyes searched for the children. When it spotted them, it let out a roar that sent snow tumbling from nearby trees.

The children raced away, darting down a steep embankment and into the woods. The leafless trees provided few hiding places and less protection from the brutal wind, which felt like little razor blades cutting Sabrina's face. Their only chance was to keep running. She and Puck scrambled down some rocks to a clearing, but it ended with a four-hundred-foot drop to the Hudson Valley below.

"Puck, I . . ."

The boy turned to her. "I know what you are going to say, and I think it's an excellent idea. I'll leave you here and save myself."

"That's not what I was going to say at all!" Sabrina shouted. "I was going to ask you if you had any ideas for getting us out of this."

"Not a one. Grimm, you usually handle the running and crying part."

"If only we had a sled," she mumbled as she looked down the steep, snowy hill.

Puck's eyes lit up. He turned around and got down on his hands and knees.

"What are you doing?" Sabrina asked.

"Climb on my back," Puck insisted. "I've got an idea."

Sabrina was all too familiar with Puck's "ideas." They usually ended in a trip to the emergency room—but with the monster lumbering down the rocky hillside behind them, there were few alternative options.

Sabrina sat on the boy's back with a leg on each side of him.

"OK, what now?"

"Grab my tusk."

"Grab your what?"

Puck turned his head toward her. His face had transformed into that of a walrus. He had two long tusks protruding from his mouth and a mustache of thick, bristly hair. His nose had vanished into his oily black face, and his eyes were large and brown. Sabrina cringed but reached around with her good arm and grabbed firmly onto one of his tusks.

"Please don't do this," she whimpered. "This is such a bad idea."

"The only bad ideas are the ones never tried," Puck said as his body began to puff up. Layers of blubber inflated under Sabrina. Puck's shirt disappeared, replaced by a super-slippery skin. "Keep your hands and feet inside the ride until it comes to a complete stop," he shouted. "Here we go!"

Puck leaped forward just as the beast reached the clearing, and his slick walrus body rocketed down the steep slope toward town.

They zipped between trees and bounced over jutting rocks. Sabrina turned back, confident the monster wouldn't follow them on this desperate flight, only to see it plowing down the hill after them, knocking over trees as if they weren't even there.

"JABBERWOCKY!"

They shot down the bank of a frozen stream, ramping off a rocky outcropping and soaring into the air, and fell for what seemed like forever. They hit the ground hard, narrowly missing the spiky branches of an oak tree. Sabrina, clutching her broken arm and gasping for air, turned again to mark the monster's progress. It, too, had used the rocky ramp and sailed into the air. Flapping its wings, it soared higher and higher; then a strong wind knocked it off course, and it slammed hard against the mountainside. Moments later, Sabrina lost sight of it completely, though she could still hear it braying in the distance.

"I think we lost it! We're safe!" she cried, just as the ground leveled off. Unfortunately, they didn't slow down. In fact, they continued zipping along as a four-lane highway of speeding cars appeared in front of them. They zoomed into traffic, spinning several times as they tried to avoid a pickup truck. The startled driver slammed on his brakes. Tires squealed and bumpers crunched. Shrill horns filled the air, but the children kept going. On the other side of the road was another steep hill, and they whipped down it, heading right for a ramshackle old barn. Its doors were

wide open, and they slid inside, crashing at last into the far wall of an empty stable.

"Personally, I think I earned every penny of that seven million dollars!" Puck said, laughing so hard that he rolled over onto his fat, blubbery side. Giggling, he transformed back into his true form—an annoying eleven-year-old boy.

Sabrina's head hurt too much for her to be angry at his recklessness. She was exhausted, and her arm felt as if it were ready to fall off. She gazed around the barn. A few bales of hay sat in the corner, and an old plow lay rusting on the ground. High on the wall, several windows were wide open, allowing the snowstorm to blow inside. It was freezing, but at least they were out of the wind.

Puck must have heard her teeth chattering, because he did something so un-Puck-like, Sabrina couldn't believe it. He got up, sat down behind her, and let his enormous fairy wings sprout from his back. Then he wrapped them around her to keep the bitter cold away. It was the first truly nice thing the so-called Trickster King had ever done for her. Instinctively she wanted to tease him for this rare moment of compassion, but she bit her tongue. Knowing Puck, he'd storm off and she'd die an ice cube.

"What was that thing?" she asked.

"It's called a Jabberwocky," Puck said. "Two tons of teeth, tail, and terror. From what I've heard, they're impossible to kill. But don't worry, Grimm: It's gone. It had its share of the Trickster King for one day."

"We need to get help," Sabrina said, shivering.

"I'm on it," Puck said. He reached into his pocket, pulled out a small wooden flute, and blew a couple of high-pitched notes. Within seconds, a swarm of little lights flooded through the open windows and surrounded the children. They looked like fireflies, but Sabrina knew better. They were Puck's pixie servants—or, as he called them, his minions—and they did whatever Puck asked of them, especially if it was mischief. They buzzed around their boy leader and waited for instructions.

"Go get the old lady," Puck said to them. "And bring me something to start a fire."

The pixies buzzed and darted out through the barn windows. Moments later, a wave of them returned carrying tree limbs and dead leaves. They arranged these in a pile in front of the children, then zipped away again. Soon, a second swarm returned carrying a single bottle of root beer, which they gently placed in Puck's hands.

"You have served me well, minions," he said, unscrewing the top and tossing it into a corner of the barn. He chugged the whole drink and tossed the bottle aside. He wiped his mouth on his sleeve.

"Was that refreshing? I'd hate for you to be thirsty. Maybe you would like a sandwich, too," Sabrina snarled.

"Keep your pants on," the boy said. "I'm trying to keep you from turning into a Grimmsicle."

He unfolded his wings, stood up, and leaned over the pile of timber. His eyes were watering, apparently from all the gassy soda, and suddenly he opened his mouth wide and belched. The burp was deep and guttural and, much to Sabrina's surprise, accompanied by a fireball that shot out of his mouth and ignited the firewood.

"I didn't know you could do that," she said.

"Oh, I'm full of surprises," the boy said proudly as a rumbling sound came from his belly. "Want to see what I can do out the other end?"

The little pixies buzzed and twittered. To Sabrina it sounded as if they were encouraging him.

"Uh, no thanks," she said, edging closer to the fire.

"Suit yourself," he said, then turned to his small servants.

The little lights let out a disappointed sound and zipped away. When they were gone, Puck wrapped his huge fairy wings around Sabrina again.

"I'm sorry we couldn't save your parents," he whispered.

Sabrina wanted to cry. She had been so close to rescuing Henry and Veronica, and they had slipped through her fingers. How was she supposed to fight the little girl in the red cloak, who obviously had magical abilities and controlled a hulking freak with a zillion teeth? Sabrina was just an ordinary eleven-year-old girl. She was powerless. She looked over her shoulder at Puck. He was a fairy—a creature of pure magic. Puck could turn into all kinds of animals, he could fly, he had pixie servants, and now, apparently, even his obnoxious bad habits were useful. The boy was overflowing with power, and it gave him a fearlessness Sabrina envied.

"I'd prefer it if we kept the heroics to ourselves," he said now, interrupting her thoughts. "The last thing I need is you yapping to everyone in town about me being a hero. I am most definitely not a hero. I'm a villain . . ."

"Of the worst kind," said Sabrina, finishing the boy's sentence.

"And don't you forget it!"

"How could I?" Sabrina asked, her voice sounding thick in her own ears. She was suddenly exhausted. "You tell me every ten minutes."

Puck didn't respond, and for a long moment the children were silent.

"Go to sleep, Grimm. I won't let anything bad happen to you," Puck said.

"And how much does that cost?"

"Don't worry. I'll put it on your tab," he replied.

2

WHEN SABRINA WOKE, SHE WAS IN A hospital room with a clunky plaster cast on her broken arm. Her little sister, Daphne, sat on the edge of her bed, busily scribbling GET WELL SOON! on the cast with a black marker.

Daphne had been through a lot in the last year and a half—both of them had. The orphanage, the insane foster families, their nasty caseworker, giants, monsters, and mayhem. Through it all, Sabrina had protected her sister the best she could, growing up fast so that Daphne wouldn't have to. It was worth it to keep the ever-present smile on her little sister's face.

"Hey, monkey," Sabrina said.

Daphne screamed with joy and hugged her sister tightly.

"Are you OK?" Sabrina asked.

"I'm fine," Daphne said, kissing her sister on each cheek.

"And Granny Relda?"

"She's good. She went to get a cup of coffee. She'll be right back."

Daphne took a step back, crossed her arms, and forced a disapproving scowl onto her face.

"You're grounded!" she said.

"What?" Despite her tears, Sabrina had to bite her lip to stop herself from laughing.

"You heard me. You're grounded."

"What for?"

"For being a jerk," Daphne said. "Mayor Charming gave us the Little Match Girl's matches. *We* were supposed to make a wish and step through the portal to save Mom and Dad *together*. But *you* ran off all willy-nilly by yourself without even knowing what you were getting into. You're lucky you weren't killed."

It was obvious that Daphne had rehearsed her lecture many times, but the little girl's sweet face and goofy overalls made it hard to take her seriously.

"This is super-serious stuff," Daphne said, noticing the grin on Sabrina's face. "This isn't funny. I'm really mad. Every time something important is happening, you run off on your own and leave me behind. I'm part of this family, too, you know."

"Daphne, I was worried you'd get hurt. You're only seven years old."

"I'm tough," she said, stomping her foot.

"Mr. Canis?" Sabrina asked, dreading the answer.

Daphne's eyes welled with tears, and Sabrina knew the old man was dead. She hugged her sister tightly, both to comfort her and to prevent the little girl from seeing her own tears. Mr. Canis was her grandmother's best friend, despite the fact that he was also the Big Bad Wolf. When Rumpelstiltskin had tried to blow a hole in the magical barrier enclosing the town, her family stopped him. Canis was caught in an explosion that destroyed her elementary school, but Sabrina had hoped he had somehow survived.

"It's going to be OK," she said.

Daphne wiped her face, then grimaced. "There's something else I need to tell you."

Sabrina's heart sank into her belly. Was someone else hurt? Had someone else died trying to save the town?

"I sort of accidentally left my marker lying around when I went to the bathroom, and Puck came in, and—"

"What did Puck do?"

Daphne closed her eyes and bit her lip. "I just want you to know it wasn't my fault," the little girl continued. "When Granny told him there was no way in the world you could pay him seven million dollars for saving your life . . . well, he got real angry. Did you really agree to that?"

"*What did he do?*"

"Don't panic, OK? Granny says it will come off eventually," Daphne whispered.

Sabrina eyed the black marker in Daphne's hand, and a bubble of fear rose in her throat. She stumbled out of bed and rushed to the bathroom in the far corner of the room. Once inside, she flicked on the light, looked into the mirror, and screamed. A thick mustache ending in fancy curlicues was drawn above her lips. On her chin was a devilish goatee, and on her forehead were the words CAPTAIN DOODIEFACE. She looked like a deranged eleven-year-old pirate. Sabrina turned on the faucet and snatched a washcloth off the rack. Once it was good and lathered with soap, she scrubbed her face until her skin was red and raw. She rinsed the suds off to see her progress and screamed again. Puck's graffiti was still there.

"*He is so dead!*" she shrieked.

"You're panicking. Don't panic," said Daphne as she stepped sheepishly into the bathroom.

"Where is that little troll?" Sabrina cried as she stomped back into the room. Puck had pulled some pretty terrible pranks in the past—tarantulas in her bed, a boa constrictor in the shower, and even Krazy Glue on her toothbrush—but this was the worst.

"If he's smart, he's hiding from the terrible wrath of Sabrina Grimm," an elderly voice said from across the room. The girls turned and found Granny Relda standing in the doorway. She was an old woman in a sky-blue dress and a matching hat with a sunflower appliqué on it. She rushed to Sabrina and wrapped her up in her arms, and Sabrina's anger dissolved. She was so happy to see the old woman that everything else lost its importance, even Puck's face graffiti.

"I saw Mom and Dad," Sabrina said. "They were in some kind of building on top of Mount Taurus. It looked kind of like a hospital. There was a little girl in a red cloak and a monster as big as a truck. Puck says it's called a Jabberwocky."

"Creepy!" Daphne cried.

"They looked fine, Granny. They were sleeping. We tried to rescue them, but the Jabberwocky set the place on fire, and then the little girl used some kind of magic ring and vanished. The place looked abandoned, but there were red handprints all over the walls. Granny, I think she's the leader of the Scarlet Hand. We should go up there right away. We might find some clues!"

"Sabrina, you've been in the hospital for two days," Granny Relda said in her light German accent.

Two days! Sabrina felt a sob rising in her throat.

"You were exhausted from the fight with Rumpelstiltskin and the broken arm," Granny said. "Your body needed a rest."

"Then we have to go up there now," Sabrina cried.

"I doubt there is anything left of the asylum," the old woman said.

"What's an asylum?" Daphne asked.

"It's a prison for crazy people," Sabrina said.

"No, it's a hospital for people struggling with mental illnesses," Granny said. "We can talk about all this later. Right now, it's time to take you home."

"But—"

Just then a nurse entered the room carrying a bouquet of exotic flowers. "Oh, look, our patient is awake," she said, "in time to receive some flowers. These just arrived."

She set the flowers on the table, and Sabrina pulled a little card off the side of the pot and read the inscription. GET WELL SOON. LOVE, JAKE.

Granny's face tightened for a moment, but then she smiled. "Must have been sent to the wrong room. Let's go, girls. We have a ride waiting for us downstairs."

Snow White was beautiful, charming, sweet, funny, and intelligent. The only thing she wasn't was subtle. She couldn't stop staring at Sabrina's mustache and goatee in the rearview mirror. After catching the woman's gaze for the hundredth time, Sabrina finally blurted out that she was the victim of another one of Puck's pranks.

Ms. White laughed so hard she snorted. "Boys will be boys," she said as she steered her car down the old country roads of Ferryport Landing. "They can be pretty immature when they're young, but they get a little better as they get older."

"Puck is over four thousand years old, Ms. White," Sabrina grumbled. "I think the odds of him getting more mature are pretty slim."

"You're probably right." The woman sighed, sharing a knowing smile with Granny Relda. "Billy is nearly five hundred, and most of the time he doesn't act a day over seven."

"So, are you two a couple now?" Daphne cooed. She hung on the back of the front seat to hear all the gossip.

Ms. White's cheeks flushed bright red. "We're just talking."

Granny Relda smiled. "I've heard the mayor has sent you flowers every day."

"Relda, you gossip! Who told you that?" Snow White demanded.

"Oh, a little bird," Granny replied.

Sabrina rolled her eyes. In a town like Ferryport Landing, filled with magical creatures, there was a good chance that an actual little bird had told her.

"When you two get married, can I be your flower girl?" Daphne begged.

Now Ms. White rolled her eyes. "I'll make you a deal, Daphne. If the mayor and I ever get married, you can be the flower girl. But you might be a very old woman. We're taking things very slowly— and besides, Billy is very busy with the election."

"Election?" Sabrina asked.

"The mayoral election," Ms. White explained. "We have one every four years—though it seems like a bit of a waste of money these days. No one ever runs against Billy."

Soon, the teacher steered her car into the Grimm family's driveway and parked. Everyone got out and said their good-byes.

"Snow, thank you so much for the ride," Granny Relda said.

"My pleasure, Relda. If you need anything, just give me a ring. Until the school is rebuilt, all I've got to keep me busy is the self-defense class. Which reminds me," she said, turning to Daphne, "will I be seeing my star pupil again this Friday?"

The little girl bowed to her, the way people do in martial arts films.

"Yes, *sensei*," she said.

"Have you been practicing your warrior face?"

The little girl clenched her hands into claws, squinted her eyes, and contorted her mouth so that she looked like she was very angry, though her overalls with a kitten sewn on the front made it all a little comical.

"Very intimidating," Snow White said. She wished Sabrina a speedy recovery before getting back in her car and driving away.

"What was all that *sensei* stuff?" Sabrina asked her little sister.

"Granny thought it was a good idea to keep me busy while you were in the hospital. She signed me up for Ms. White's Bad Apples self-defense class at the community center. I've only gone once, but she says I'm fierce. She's been teaching me how to do a warrior face. It lets an attacker know that you mean business," Daphne explained.

"It looked like you wanted to let the attacker know you're constipated," Sabrina said.

"What does *constipated* mean?" Daphne asked.

Sabrina leaned over, cupped her hand around her sister's ear, and whispered the definition to her.

The little girl stepped back and crinkled up her nose. "You're gross."

Granny dug in her handbag for her key ring. It had hundreds of keys on it, which she quickly sorted through to find the ones that fit the dozen locks on the front door. When she was finished with the keys, she knocked three times on the door and said, "We're home." The last magical lock slid open, and the family hurried inside the house and out of the cold.

Daphne helped Sabrina out of her coat and boots. With her broken arm in its clunky cast, she realized there were a few things she wouldn't be able to do on her own. She didn't like being dependent. Having Daphne take care of her made her feel like a baby. Still, there was something she could do to help everyone, and she couldn't wait to get started. She made a beeline for the enormous bookshelves in the living room. They housed the family's collection of journals—clothbound records of everything every Grimm had experienced since Jacob and Wilhelm Grimm had arrived in the town more than two hundred years earlier. Sabrina was sure there would be something in them about a little girl in red and her pet monster. But before she could grab a single volume, her grandmother stepped in her way.

"Uh-uh. No detective work today. You're going straight to bed and getting some rest."

"Rest? I've been asleep for two days," Sabrina complained. "I can rest when Mom and Dad are safe at home."

The old woman shook her head. "Upstairs," she said.

Sabrina scowled and stomped up the steps to her room. Granny Relda and Daphne followed and helped her out of her clothes. The whole experience was humiliating. Sabrina couldn't even put on her own pajamas without help. Climbing into bed was equally difficult, and when her grandmother laid heavy quilts on her, she knew that getting out again was going to be a real challenge.

"Reading one of the journals might make me sleepy," Sabrina said as her grandmother added another blanket to the mountain of down quilts.

Granny ignored her. "Are you warm enough?"

"Yes! You could bake a turkey under here," the girl said, struggling to free herself.

Elvis peeked around the doorjamb.

"Elvis!" Sabrina called. "Come here, boy! Help me escape!"

The family's two-hundred-pound Great Dane let out a soft whine. Despite his imposing figure and a face that said "I can eat you in one bite," the dog had a sensitive, loving nature. He was incredibly playful and affectionate with the girls, and normally he would have leaped onto the bed and covered Sabrina in happy kisses. There was something wrong.

"What's with him?" Sabrina asked.

"He's pouting," Granny Relda said stiffly.

"Pouting? Why?"

"Young man, get in here and say hello," Granny insisted.

Elvis snorted and reluctantly stepped out from behind the door. He was wearing a green vest, white booties, a saggy red Santa hat with furry white trim, and a long white beard under his chin. When he was in full view, he dropped his head and whined.

"What did you do to him?" Sabrina asked.

"It's his holiday outfit," Daphne said.

Elvis whined.

"You poor pathetic boy," Sabrina said.

"I think he looks very handsome. He's my handsome little Christmas baby."

"He's one miserable baby," Sabrina said, laughing.

"I've been working on that costume for days!" Granny exclaimed. Elvis dropped his head and whined again.

"OK," Granny said, surrendering. "Take it off him."

Elvis ran around in circles, happily knocking Daphne to the floor as she tried to remove his vest and hat. He gave her a slobbery lick on the face when she succeeded in removing his white beard. She handed it to Sabrina. "You want this? It'll hide the goatee."

Sabrina frowned and shrank down so that the covers were just beneath her nose. "Puck is so dead."

"Your sister's bunking with me tonight, so you've got the room all to yourself," Granny said.

"What about Mom and Dad?"

"Your parents are fine. You said yourself that they looked as if they had been sleeping the whole time. For now, I don't believe confronting the girl and her Jabberwocky is wise."

Sabrina couldn't believe her ears. Granny Relda was turning down a mystery, and one that involved her own flesh and blood.

"You and your sister don't need to be snooping with that thing running around," Granny said, seemingly reading Sabrina's mind. "Promise me you will not go back, Sabrina."

"I don't understand why you won't even go up there," Sabrina said.

"Promise me," the old woman demanded.

"She promises," Daphne said. "We won't go up there."

Satisfied, Granny led Daphne and Elvis into the hallway. When she reached the doorway, she turned, flipped off the light, and stood in the darkness watching Sabrina.

"Mom and Dad need us," Sabrina said, feeling her anger rise in her throat.

"I can't lose you, *liebling*," the old woman said quietly before she closed the door. "I've already lost too many."

Sabrina lay in bed for hours brooding. Was her grandmother really going to ignore everything Sabrina had discovered? She'd seen her mother and father. She knew what their kidnapper looked like. She'd found the location of their kidnapper. Why wasn't Granny Relda jumping into action?

The answer, whatever it was, didn't matter. Henry and Veronica were with a lunatic and a monster. They needed to be rescued. Sabrina would have to do it on her own.

It felt like hours before Sabrina wiggled free of her blanket cocoon. The only upside of all the effort was that by the time she got downstairs she was confident everyone was asleep.

She tiptoed through the house, avoiding creaky floorboards and squeaky doors. Being in the foster care system had taught her how to sneak; she could creep past someone without them ever knowing. Once in the living room, she reached over and flipped on a table lamp. Elvis was lying on the couch, a place he knew very well he was not supposed to be. He cocked his head with a guilty look.

"If you don't say anything, I won't say anything," Sabrina whispered. The big dog seemed OK with the deal. He plopped his huge noggin back down on a cushion and promptly fell asleep.

The bookshelves held the family journals, but they were also the home of the largest collection of fairy-tale stories and studies Sabrina had ever seen. It included such volumes as *The Seven People You Meet in Oz*, *Cheap Eats in Wonderland*, and a heavy one called *The Paul Bunyan Diet*. Granny wasn't much of a housekeeper, so the library spilled onto the floors and into the other rooms. Some books held up wobbly tables; others had literally been swept under the rug. Sabrina had once found a book inside the toilet tank. She reached over and scooped up as many family journals as her good arm would hold, then crossed into the dining room and placed them on the table. She eased into a chair and sat down to read. *Someone in this family has to know something about the girl in the red cloak and her Jabberwocky.*

She found her first reference to the monster in her great-great-great-great-grandfather Wilhelm's logs during his crossing of the Atlantic. He and his brother had brought the Everafters to America to help them escape persecution, and from his entries, Sabrina could see it hadn't been an easy voyage.

July 17th, 1805

I'm contemplating turning back. The voyage is already fraught with disaster. Crossing the Atlantic with a ship full of fairy-tale creatures is a difficult enough task, but things got out of hand today when the Jabberwockies got loose and ran amok. I curse myself for putting so much stock in the Queen of Hearts's demands. She insisted the beasts could be domesticated, but the woman is a fool. The trouble began only fifteen leagues out from shore. There were ten of the beasts, and together they killed a dozen human seamen before Lancelot and Robin Hood drove them into the hold of the ship. The Black Knight went down with the Vorpal blade and killed nine of them. We managed to get one back into its cage, but the damage is done. We tossed the dead things overboard. If the sharks can tolerate the meat, they're welcome to it.

"What's the Vorpal blade?" Sabrina whispered to herself, but there wasn't another mention of it in the logs. Sabrina searched the other journals but found nothing, except in two entries by her great-great-grandfather Spaulding Grimm.

March 9th, 1929

When the Lilliputians came to me with the news, I hoped it was just more of their usual mischief, but they were right—the Jabberwocky has escaped and is roaming the forest. The magic mirror has informed me that the beasts hibernate for great periods of time, and with winter coming we might be saved from too much carnage, but finding the creature will prove difficult. Like my grandfather, I have turned to the Black Knight. The man seems to lack fear. I gave him the Vorpal blade and my prayers.

March 11th, 1929

The Black Knight has betrayed me. Instead of hunting and killing the Jabberwocky, he used the Vorpal blade to cut a hole in the magical barrier that surrounds the town! I was a fool! I should have known the blade could cut through anything, but my desperate desire to find the monster blinded me to the consequences, and to his history of double dealings. The knight has escaped into the world of humans, but for some reason he left the sword behind. I found it lying nearby, thank heaven! It's the only thing that can kill a Jabberwocky, but it will do me little good. There is no one in this town brave enough to go after the monster, and no one I trust with the blade. I fear I will have to turn to Baba Yaga for assistance. Who knows what price she'll ask for, but it will have to be paid. The monster must be caged and the sword destroyed—the Blue Fairy will help, I'm sure. I can't let something this powerful exist.

Sabrina closed the journal and looked at the clock on the wall. After three hours of reading, sleep was creeping up on her. She wondered if closing her eyes for a moment or two might help. She rested her head on the dining room table, but a minute later someone said, "Time to wake up." Sabrina bolted upright in her chair and glanced around the dining room. Sitting at the opposite end of the table was the girl in the red cloak. The Jabberwocky was seated next to her, breathing so heavily that Sabrina could feel it from across the room. The two intruders hovered over a filthy tea set laid out on the table. The little girl poured a thick, stringy substance into two cups and set one in front of the monster. Its teeth gnashed, and a rope of drool fell out of its mouth.

"We're having a tea party," the little girl said to Sabrina. She poured a third cup and slid it across the table. Whatever was in it was bubbling and black.

"How did you get in here?" Sabrina choked out. Fear was crawling up her throat.

The little girl in red giggled. The sound echoed around the room.

Suddenly, Henry and Veronica materialized into empty seats. They looked terrified.

"Sabrina, you have to save us," her father said.

"You're our only hope," her mother cried.

"I'm trying," Sabrina said.

"They don't belong to you anymore," the girl in red said. "I found them. They're mine."

The Jabberwocky tossed the table aside, sending the tea set smashing to the floor. It leaped forward and wrapped its huge talons around Sabrina's neck.

And then Sabrina woke up. Her mom and dad, the Jabberwocky, and the girl in red were gone. She sat silently for a moment, struggling to catch her breath. She glanced down at the journals in front of her, noticing that her grandfather's journal was flipped open. There was something very small written at the bottom of one of the pages. She strained to read it.

Ferryport Landing Asylum Patient List—1955
The Mad Hatter—diagnosis: schizophrenia
Chicken Little—diagnosis: panic attacks
Hansel—diagnosis: severe eating disorder
The White Rabbit—diagnosis: obsessive-compulsive disorder
The Old Woman Who Lived in a Shoe—diagnosis: exhaustion
Ichabod Crane—diagnosis: night terrors
Little Red Riding Hood—diagnosis: psychosis with delusions and hallucinations, homicidal tendencies

Sabrina's heart rose up into her throat. The little girl in the red cloak was Little Red Riding Hood! Now that it was right in front of her, she felt stupid. *How did I not figure that out?* But how could she have? She'd read the story. Little Red Riding Hood was a sweet girl, a victim! She wasn't evil. Why would she kidnap Henry and Veronica Grimm? Why would she be involved with the Scarlet Hand?

Sabrina leaped from her chair and hurried through the house, back up the steps, and down the hall to Granny's room. She did her best to open the door without causing it to creak and found her sister sound asleep next to their grandmother. Sabrina rushed to her side and gently shook the little girl awake.

"What's wrong?" Daphne whispered as she rubbed the sleep from the corners of her eyes.

"You were mad at me for not including you, right?" Sabrina said.

Her little sister nodded.

"Then get up. We've got work to do."

3

YOU PROMISED GRANNY YOU WOULDN'T GO back to that place!" Daphne said as the girls rushed down the hallway.

"No, *you* promised," Sabrina said.

The little girl stepped in front of her and crossed her arms defiantly. "I won't let you go!"

"Daphne, I know who kidnapped our parents," Sabrina said.

Her sister gasped. "Who?"

"Little Red Riding Hood."

"Uh-uh!" Daphne cried.

"I know it sounds crazy, but it's true. They were being kept in the asylum Puck and I discovered—the same asylum where Red Riding Hood was a patient."

"But Granny says it burned down," Daphne argued.

"I know, but there might be clues that survived that will tell us where the little nutcase took Mom and Dad." Sabrina stepped around her sister and continued down the hallway.

"We should wait until morning. Maybe we can convince Granny to take us up there herself," the little girl said.

"You saw how she reacted. She's not going to go anywhere near that place. Besides, she's very sad about Mr. Canis. I think maybe she needs a break from detective work. Unfortunately, we don't have time to wait until she feels better. Every minute that goes by is another minute Red Riding Hood has for taking Mom and Dad farther away. She's already got a head start on us."

"But—"

"Daphne, listen!" Sabrina interrupted. "I'm bringing Mom and Dad home with or without you. They need us, and if I have to break a few rules to rescue them, then rules are going to get broken."

"What about the Jabberwocky thing?"

"I'll deal with that if and when I have to," Sabrina said, trying to sound confident.

Her sister's doubtful expression told her the words didn't sound as convincing as she'd hoped. "We should at least take Puck with us," Daphne demanded.

"No way!" Sabrina said. Her anger at the boy felt almost physical, like it might bubble over inside her body and pour out her ears.

"Yes way," Daphne insisted. "If you're going to make me break a promise to Granny, then you're going to have to let him come along."

"Then I'll go on my own," Sabrina snapped.

"And I will scream at the top of my lungs and wake Granny before you get a chance to go."

"You wouldn't."

"Try me!"

Sabrina snarled. "Fine!" she said as she marched to Puck's bedroom door. On it was a crude drawing of a crocodile that read INTRUDERS WILL B EATIN. Ignoring the sign, Sabrina turned the doorknob and dragged her sister into the room.

As always, the sight of Puck's bedroom took Sabrina's breath away. It was every little boy's fantasy come to life, but it wasn't exactly a room. In fact, the only thing about it that even remotely resembled a bedroom was the door that led to it from the hallway. Where the ceiling should have been was an open night sky filled with thousands of twinkling stars. An alligator floated lazily in the lagoon nearby, and a roller coaster rolled along a track above their heads. An ice-cream truck sat parked on the shore with discarded cones scattered everywhere. There was a wrestling ring set up off to the right, where a kangaroo wearing gym shorts and boxing gloves slumbered peacefully. A mechanical bull splattered with eggs was set up to the left.

Puck was nowhere in sight. Sabrina shouted for the boy, but

there was no reply except for the crickets that chirped in the surrounding forest.

"Should we look for him?" Daphne asked.

Sabrina shook her head. "The last time we barged in here, we wound up in a vat of glue and pickles," she said. She was still having trouble getting the gunk out of her hair. No, she had a better way to get his attention. "Hey, ugly! We need to talk!"

"Maybe he's busy," Daphne said.

"Busy doing what? Picking his nose?"

Just then a spotlight illuminated a book lying on the beach by the lagoon.

"Puck, what's going on?" Sabrina said, suspiciously.

Puck didn't reply.

"I want to see what it is," Daphne said and she marched to the lagoon and snatched the book off the sand. She flipped it open before Sabrina could stop her, then immediately put the palm of her hand into her mouth and bit down hard. She always did this when she was excited. Sabrina walked over to see what was so interesting and noticed that the book was filled with page after page of cute baby animal pictures cut from magazines and books. There were puppies playing with kittens, little foxes peeking their heads out of bushes, a pony racing through a field with its mother, little bunny rabbits nibbling lettuce, and precious white-furred baby seals frolicking on a beach. Sabrina thought her heart might melt.

"I could just eat them up!" Daphne exclaimed.

And that was when the rope whipped around their legs, flipped them upside down, and yanked them high into the air. They hung helpless above the ground with no way to free themselves.

"*Puck!*" the girls screamed.

The fairy boy stepped out from behind a row of trees. He was wearing a green camouflage helmet of the kind Sabrina had seen on soldiers in old war movies. He had on his usual filthy green hooded sweatshirt and ratty jeans, but they were covered in medals and ribbons as if he were a dirty five-star general. Spilling out of the woods behind him came a dozen chattering chimpanzees, each wearing the same helmet as their leader and bright-red overalls. They held water balloons in their hairy hands, and all looked at the swinging girls eagerly.

Puck walked to a small table where an old record player was sitting. He lifted the needle and set it down on the record. A rousing patriotic song filled the air.

"Our plan has worked, men!" Puck shouted over the music. "I told you our enemy could not resist photographs of cute baby animals!"

"Puck, get us down now!" Sabrina demanded. The blood was racing into her broken arm and making it throb with pain.

"Keep your distance, men. Don't be fooled into believing that our enemies are helpless. These 'girls,' as they call themselves, are a crafty bunch. I've seen inside the thing they call a 'purse.' It is filled with all kinds of toxic sprays and pointy things they wouldn't hesitate to unleash on us."

The chimps looked at him with great respect.

"Now, unfortunately, the laws of war prohibit us from killing these two, but I believe we can make examples out of them. And that will deliver a clear message to the rest of their kind."

One of the chimpanzees raced to his side and handed him a fat, sloshy water balloon.

"Puck! Don't you dare!" Sabrina warned.

"Oh, but I do dare, Captain Doodieface," Puck said, turning to his army. "Men, fire at will!"

The first wave of balloons hit Sabrina in the chest and splattered onto Daphne's face, but instead of drenching them in water, they covered the girls in something that smelled a lot like a combination of mayonnaise and grape jelly. The second wave was relentless, and the balloons kept coming until the chimps ran out of ammunition. By that time, the girls were covered from head to toe.

Puck pulled his wooden sword from his belt and stepped over to his prisoners. He poked Sabrina in the side with the tip.

"Now you know what happens to people who do not pay their debts," Puck said.

"One of these days I'm going to get my revenge, fairy boy,"

Sabrina said. "You won't know when it's coming, but it'll happen when you least expect it."

"Your threats are boring me, Captain. B-O-R-N-G, boring!"

"*I am going to—*"

"Puck, we were just thinking of sneaking out and getting into some trouble," Daphne said, interrupting her sister's tirade. "We thought you'd like to come along."

The boy cocked an eyebrow. "What kind of trouble?"

"We want to go back up to the asylum and look for clues about our parents."

"*Boring!*" Puck said, then let out a loud yawn.

"This is important!" Sabrina insisted.

"Which makes it even more boring," Puck said. "I've got better things to do."

"Like what?" Sabrina snapped.

"Staring at my belly button, for one! Then there're toenails to chew off, and a few scabs that need my attention. The day is packed."

"When we're finished, we could go to the overpass and toss rotten tomatoes at passing cars," Daphne offered.

Puck's eyes lit up. "Cut them down, men."

After the girls got cleaned up and put on some warm clothing, the trio was off, soaring high above the ground thanks to Puck's wings. The little snow-covered town lay sleeping, unaware that a flying boy and two young girls were floating high above. As angry as Sabrina was at Puck, she found herself envying him once again. Puck had powers, and those powers made him useful. If only she could do something special, too.

"I still can't believe Little Red Riding Hood kidnapped Mom and Dad," Daphne said. "She's the hero of that story."

"Well, clearly she's changed," Sabrina said. "She and the Jabberwocky nearly killed us."

"Nearly killed *you*," Puck argued. "I beat the stuffing out of that overgrown lizard."

Sabrina rolled her eyes, then spotted the hospital below.

"There it is," she said, pointing at the burned-out shell. Part of the roof was still intact, and much of the right wing of the hospital was still standing, but otherwise the place was in ruins.

"There's not much left, Grimm," Puck said as he set the girls at what was once the asylum's front door.

"Where do we start?" Daphne asked.

"In the parts that are still standing," Sabrina said.

Puck took out his little flute and blew a few notes. Soon, the children were surrounded by thousands of pixies. "Minions, we need some light."

Instantly, the glow that seemed to burn from within the little beings grew brighter and brighter. The pixies went from looking like fireflies to looking like light bulbs, and their dazzling radiance illuminated the entire top of the mountain.

"Nice trick," Sabrina said as she took her first step into the ruins. Everywhere she looked she saw scorched papers and roasted furniture. She led the others from room to room, searching for anything that might be about Red Riding Hood. Unfortunately, most of the file cabinets were empty or had been welded shut by the flames. One tiny room, lined with soft, padded walls, was untouched by the fire. A crumpled white jacket with dozens of buckles and belts lay on the floor—a straitjacket. It was a creepy reminder of the building's history.

"Well, this was an enormous waste of time," Puck grumbled after the last of the rooms was explored. "Let's go to the overpass. Those rotten tomatoes aren't going to throw themselves."

"I agree," Daphne said. "I am totally freaked out, anyway."

Sabrina's heart sank. The others were right. Anything that might have pointed toward her parents' location was ash. She was so disappointed. Tears threatened to escape her eyes, so she turned and marched back the way they had come, not wanting Puck or Daphne to see.

"Slow down," Daphne said. "I'm scared."

"There's nothing in here that's going to get you. Stop being a baby!" Sabrina said over her shoulder.

Suddenly, there was a horrible crashing sound and a shout from her sister. Sabrina spun around to find a hole in the floor where Daphne had just stood. The burnt boards had collapsed beneath her weight and dropped her into the darkness below.

"Daphne!"

There was a long, horrible silence until she heard her sister's voice.

"Sabrina?"

"Are you OK?"

"Yes. Sabrina?"

"What?"

"I hate you!" the little girl screamed.

Puck grabbed onto the back of Sabrina's coat, and together they jumped into the hole. Though she couldn't see his wings, Sabrina felt them flutter to slow their descent. The two floated to the floor below, followed by several glowing pixies. Daphne was unharmed but covered in dust. Sabrina reached out to help the little girl up, but her sister looked at the offered hand as if it were a snake. She snarled, then stood up on her own.

"Sabrina Grimm! Of all the stupid ideas you've ever had, this is the stupidest. We could get killed in here!"

Sabrina didn't mean to ignore her sister's anger, but now that she could see the room, she was dumbfounded. It was a dungeon, with high granite walls. In one corner a pair of enormous chains were fastened to the rock. Against the opposite wall leaned a large antique mirror, its reflective surface destroyed. Scorched shards of glass littered the floor beneath it. But the oddest of the room's furnishings was the baby crib. It was made from solid oak and had a little blue blanket inside, along with a pacifier and a fluffy white teddy bear.

"What is all this?" Puck asked.

"Red Riding Hood mentioned something about having a baby brother," Sabrina said. "I thought she was just delusional, but maybe it's true. Could she have stolen someone's child just like she stole Mom and Dad?"

Daphne opened the top drawer of a small file cabinet in the far corner of the room and yanked out a collection of aging folders. "Hey! I found something."

Sabrina rushed to her side, grabbed the files, and flipped through them. Soon she came upon one marked PATIENT 67— LITTLE RED RIDING HOOD. As she leafed through it, a page fell onto the floor. She picked it up and noticed it was a crayon drawing of a family. There was a father, a mother holding a baby, a grandmother, a small child in a red cloak, a hideous monster that could only be the Jabberwocky, and a ferocious-looking dog as big as a man.

"This is her medical file," Sabrina said.

"Good. Can we get out of here now?" Daphne asked. "I'm totally freaked out, and my butt hurts."

"We can't go yet. There could be more clues down here," Sabrina argued.

Just then a man stepped out of the shadows. He was tall and wore a long overcoat. He was about her father's age, with milky blue eyes, shaggy blond hair, and a nose that had been broken in three places. Around his neck were a dozen necklaces and amulets. Every one of his fingers had a ring on it.

"Girls, I need that file," he said as he stepped toward them.

Puck leaped between the girls and the stranger, then pulled his sword from his belt. He waved it in the man's face and bonked him on the nose with its tip.

"I'm going to give you to the count of three to run off, or you're going to get a bellyful of steel. One . . ." Puck turned to face Sabrina with an embarrassed expression. "What comes after one?"

"Two." Sabrina groaned.

Puck nodded. "Two!"

"Listen, there's been a big misunderstanding," the man said.

"Three!" Puck looked over at Sabrina to make sure he was correct. She nodded at him, and he burst into action, quickly bringing his sword down on the man's hand.

"Oww!" the stranger cried. "Cut it out with the sword, kid!"

"I am Puck, son of Oberon, otherwise known as the Trickster King, spiritual leader of hooligans, good-for-nothings, and punks," he cried as he landed a kick on the stranger's rear and

pushed him to the ground. Puck leaned over his victim, waving the sword in his face. "Had enough?" he asked.

The strange man fumbled into the pockets of his coat. It was then that Sabrina noticed it had dozens of pockets sewn into it. The man removed something silver and shiny. He uttered a few nonsensical words, and suddenly everything in Sabrina's vision started to shimmer. She felt queasy, as if she were seasick, and then something unbelievable happened. The man's shadow moved of its own accord. It pulled itself off the ground with a loud *slurp!* and walked around erratically as if it were an actual person shaking off a case of the dizzies. When it seemed to have finally gotten its bearings, it stepped between Puck and the stranger and put up its hands in a boxing stance.

The shadow rushed forward to attack, but Puck blocked its punches, then threw a few of his own. Unfortunately, the counterattack didn't faze the shadow at all; the boy's fists passed harmlessly through the spirit's body. Startled, Puck fell backward, allowing the shadow to get the upper hand. It leaped into the air, did a backflip over the boy, and landed behind him. A swift kick to the Trickster King's rump followed. The boy yelped, then swooped over to Daphne and Sabrina, yanked them off the ground, and zipped up through the hole and into the room above. The shadow man followed, grabbing Sabrina's feet and forcing Puck to crash into a wall. Sabrina and Daphne tumbled roughly to the floor.

Puck and the shadow went back to fighting, and the shadow's master, the stranger, flew up through the hole, landed in the room, and headed straight for the girls.

"Here he comes. What do we do?" Daphne asked.

Sabrina looked down at the chunks of burnt furniture scattered about. She grabbed a blackened chair leg and flung it at the stranger, hitting him in the ribs.

"Oww!" he cried.

Daphne did the same, snatching another charred piece of wood and hurling it in the man's direction. Unfortunately, her aim was way off and she hit Puck instead.

"Hey! What's the big idea?" the boy complained.

"We're trying to help," Sabrina said.

"Well, stop trying so hard," Puck shouted. "Your help hurts!"

"This isn't working," Daphne said, and before Sabrina could stop her, the little girl raced up to the stranger and came to a stop.

"First you bow to your opponent," Daphne said as she bowed low.

"What's this?" the man asked.

"Daphne, get away from him!"

The little girl ignored her sister's warning. "Move into offensive stance," she said, stepping forward with her left leg and shifting her body so that her torso was turned perpendicular to her opponent. She raised her fists.

The stranger looked slightly amused.

"Present your warrior face," Daphne said, crinkling up her nose and eyes and then screaming "*Argggghhhh!*"

"All right, everyone has to calm down," the stranger said. "If you let me explain—"

"Deliver attack!" Daphne yelled. She cried, "*Hiya!*" and kicked him in the shin. He groaned in pain and bent down to hold his sore leg.

"Deliver secondary attack," the little girl said. She spun around in a complete circle and caught the man's other leg with a sweeping kick. He fell over as if he had been chopped down with an ax.

The little girl continued kicking the man as he curled up in a ball to avoid her vicious feet. "Uh, hello . . . I could use some help," Daphne said to her sister.

Sabrina shook off her surprise, and together they took turns kicking the stranger.

The man cried out for help, and his shadow immediately stopped fighting with Puck. It rushed to his side and grabbed Daphne and Sabrina in its arms. The girls fought against its icy grip, but it was too strong, and while they struggled, the stranger managed to get to his feet.

"All right, I've had just about all I'm going to take from you kids," the man growled as he reached into his pocket once again.

Before he could pull out another weapon, Puck swooped down and snatched the girls by the backs of their coats.

"This party is over!" he said, then soared into the night sky. Undeterred, the shadow sailed after them, grabbed at Sabrina with its horrible hands, yanked the medical file from under her arm, and flew away. Sabrina cried out and begged Puck to go back for it, but he refused.

As they flew toward home, Sabrina looked down at the cold black forest. It might have been a tear in her eye, or the reflection of the moon, but for a second she could have sworn she saw someone racing through the woods below at an incredible speed— someone with a shock of white hair. *It's late*, she told herself, *and it's been a long, hard day.*

4

PUCK AND DAPHNE WERE ALREADY AT THE dining room table when Sabrina came down for breakfast. With forks and knives in hand, they pounded on the table. "We want to eat! We want to eat!" Elvis barked along with their demands.

Sabrina took a seat just as Granny Relda entered the room carrying several plates of food. She set them on the table and glanced at Sabrina.

"*Liebling*! You look like you were up all night," she said.

"Slept like a baby," Sabrina lied. She knew she looked tired. When she'd brushed her teeth earlier that morning, she'd seen the dark circles under her bloodshot eyes. The stubborn black-marker mustache and goatee weren't helping her appearance, either. Ten minutes of intense scrubbing hadn't made a difference.

Granny raised a suspicious eyebrow but said nothing, zipping back into the kitchen for more food. Soon, every inch of table was overflowing with flapjacks, toast, scrambled eggs, waffles, sausages, oatmeal, French toast, fruit, and yogurt. Best of all, it was normal food. Granny's odd culinary tastes usually included black spaghetti, tofu waffles, daffodil gravy, porcupine stew, and cream-of-skunk-cabbage soup.

"What's all this for?" Sabrina asked as the lovely aromas enveloped her.

"We're celebrating your return from the hospital, of course," Granny said, as she served the girl a heaping spoonful of scrambled eggs, some link sausages, a couple of pancakes, and a few slices of apple. She took Sabrina's fork and knife and cut up the meal so Sabrina could easily eat it with one hand. Then she poured maple syrup over all of it. Sabrina took a bite and was surprised to find that it was actually real maple syrup and not some exotic concoction the woman had brought back from Kathmandu or Timbuktu or one of the other zillion places she had visited.

Daphne impaled a pancake on her fork and flipped it into the air. Elvis caught it midair and wolfed it down without chewing. Then the little girl took a pancake for herself and shoved the whole thing into her mouth. Sabrina couldn't tell whether the dog or her sister had worse table manners. Still, neither was as disgusting as Puck. He scooped up eggs with his bare hands and crammed them into his mouth. Granny smacked his hand with a serving spoon when he tried to do the same thing with the oatmeal.

"Well, so much for seconds," Sabrina grumbled.

"I have a very important announcement to make," Puck said, wiping his greasy mitts on the front of his green hoodie.

Granny raised her eyes in surprise. "Don't keep us waiting."

"As all of you know, I have been saving your lives a lot lately. It seems every time I turn around you three are a breath away from the grave. Unfortunately, it is the opinion of some people in this house that I cannot charge for my skills, so I hereby announce that I am retiring."

"Retiring?"

"Yes, being a hero was never a good fit. I happen to be a villain—"

"Of the worst kind," the Grimms said. "We know, we know!"

Puck scowled. "I'm going back to being a full-time evildoer, which, unfortunately, means that since I'm not saving your lives anymore, you're all as good as dead. But a villain has to draw the line somewhere! Bad guys do not save people from the jaws of doom, at least not for free! Bad guys push people into them."

Granny Relda smiled. "But you're so good at saving us."

Puck shook his spoon at her. "Don't even joke about that, old lady. I'm serious. I'm going to have to do an awful lot of bad stuff just to balance out all the heroism."

"Oh, so you did this when you were being a saint," Sabrina said, pointing at the doodles on her face.

"I could have tattooed it, Captain!" Puck said. "I regret holding back."

Sabrina threw down her fork and rose to her feet. "Come here and let me show you how bad I can be!"

Puck leaped up, spun around on his heels, and morphed into a parrot. He hopped onto Daphne's shoulder and shrieked, "Shiver me timbers, it's Captain Doodieface, scourge of the smelly seas!"

"Children!" Granny cried.

Just then a series of short honks followed by a long impatient blast came from outside.

"Who's that?" Daphne asked.

"Oh my, he's early. Children, let's hurry and get our coats on," Granny said.

Puck morphed back into a boy. "Where are we going?"

"To the opening ceremony for the new elementary school. Ms. White invited us," Granny said. "Everyone will be there."

"What new school? The old one just blew up three days ago," Sabrina said. Granny ignored her and hurried to the closet for the coats.

Daphne snatched a handful of pancakes and wrapped them around some link sausages. She dipped them all into the syrup on her plate and shoved them into her pants pocket.

"That's going to smell fantastic later," Sabrina said.

"It's better to be smelly than hungry," Daphne said matter-of-factly as she tried to put on her mittens with sticky fingers.

Puck crossed his arms in a huff. "I just want to be clear. If a monster attacks while we're at this ceremony, I am not going to get in its way. In fact, I might actually help drive the crowd into a frenzy. Are you sure you want me to go, old lady?"

"We'll take our chances," Granny Relda said.

Elvis trotted into the room. Seeing that everyone was leaving, he began to whine. Daphne rushed to the big dog and hugged him.

"Honey baby, sweetheart, we wouldn't leave you," she assured the Great Dane, and gave him a big smooch on his lips. Elvis licked the girl's maple syrup–covered face and then went to work stealing the pancakes from her pocket. Daphne squirmed away from the furry breakfast bandit. "Hey, get your own, you traitor."

"Come here, boy," Granny said, and the big dog darted to her. The old woman quickly dressed him in his Christmas vest and hat before he could get away. Elvis dropped his head and sighed. "Don't be a baby. It's cold out there."

"And what are we going to do about you?" she asked, cupping her hand under Sabrina's chin and eyeing her face closely. "Honestly, Puck. This time you've gone too far."

"I'm in a foul mood, old lady," Puck cried. "Don't try to cheer me up with compliments."

Granny pulled a bright orange toboggan hat out of the closet and pulled it down until it covered the writing on Sabrina's forehead. Then she wrapped an itchy wool scarf around the girl's face all the way up past her nose. "Perfect!" the old woman declared.

Once everyone was ready, the family stepped outside. A bright yellow taxicab with fuzzy dice hanging from the rearview mirror was parked in the driveway. Sitting in the front seat was an incredibly old man with a long white beard. His head was tilted back, and even from the porch the girls could hear his loud, raspy snores.

Granny stepped over to his window and tapped on it several times. When this proved ineffective, she knocked even harder. Still the man dozed away. Finally, Granny opened the front door and pushed down on the car's horn. The blast shocked the old man, and he jumped in his seat.

"Great Jehoshaphat!" he cried.

"Mr. Van Winkle, we're ready to go," Granny Relda said.

The tired old man rubbed the sleep out of his eyes and climbed out of the car. He wore a black bomber jacket and slacks. He looked like some of the cab drivers in New York City, except for the bristly white beard that hung down to his ankles.

"You didn't say anything about a dog," he grumbled.

"Mr. Van Winkle, this is Elvis. He's perfectly tame," Granny Relda insisted, ushering Elvis, Daphne, and Puck into the back of the cab, squeezing in after them, and leaving the front seat for Sabrina.

"Has he got all his shots?" the driver moaned.

"Have *you?*" Daphne asked, covering Elvis's ears with her hands so he wouldn't hear the driver's comments. "Don't listen to the mean man."

"Fine, bring the mongrel. But if he wrecks my cab, you're going to have to pay for the damage," Mr. Van Winkle griped. Sabrina looked the car over as she walked around to the passenger side. It was a collage of scratches, dents, and dings. Duct tape covered every inch of it. It reminded Sabrina of the kind of car that's slammed into walls to check for safety. When she looked inside, she half expected to see a crash-test dummy in the passenger seat. There was nothing that Elvis could do to the four-wheeled death trap that the driver hadn't done already.

When they were all inside, Elvis's big head popped up over the front seat and he sniffed the air wildly. The little old man had a greasy sack on the dashboard that smelled of hot peppers and mozzarella. Elvis rested his head on the driver's shoulder and eyed the bag hungrily, letting out a whimper.

"Not a chance, fleabag. That's my lunch," Mr. Van Winkle said before he turned his attention to Sabrina. Her scarf had slipped down, revealing her mustache and goatee. "I've never had a pirate in my cab before."

Puck laughed so hard he snorted.

Sabrina frowned and adjusted her scarf.

"Where to?" the cabbie asked.

"We're going to the new school," Granny Relda explained.

"We'll be there in a flash," Mr. Van Winkle said. He put his keys into the ignition and turned on the engine. Then nothing. For some time Sabrina thought the old man was thinking about a good route, or maybe waiting for traffic to pass so he could back out. But when five minutes had elapsed, Sabrina looked over to see she was wrong.

"He's asleep again," she said.

Granny leaned forward and eyed the man. "Give him a little poke in the arm."

Sabrina nudged his shoulder, but it didn't wake the old man.

"Try the horn," Granny Relda said.

Sabrina pushed down on the car horn, and the old man awoke with a start. "For the love of Pete!" he cried. He rubbed his eyes once more. "Where to?"

"The new school," Granny answered patiently.

The driver threw the car into reverse and pumped the gas. They were off.

"So you two are the famous Sabrina and Daphne Grimm, huh?" asked the cabbie. "Heard a lot about'cha. Word is you two killed a giant, took down Rumpelstiltskin, and went head-to-head with a Jabberwocky. Tough kids. Never heard of anyone walking away from one of those things without the Vorpal blade."

"You've heard of the Vorpal blade?" Sabrina asked, remembering her research from the night before.

"Yep, that's the only thing that can kill a Jabberwocky, from what I hear," the driver said.

"Any idea where we could get one?"

The driver chuckled. "It's not like they sell them at Walmart. No, there was only one Vorpal blade, and from what I hear it's lost."

Sabrina frowned.

"So you're an Everafter?" Daphne asked.

"Sure, I'm Rip Van Winkle," the driver said. "You ever hear of me?"

Daphne squealed. Meeting the man behind the famous Washington Irving story was like meeting a movie star to the seven-year-old girl.

"I read about you in the orphanage library," she said. "You fell asleep for a hundred years, and when you woke up everything was different. How did it feel to sleep that long?"

There was no answer. Sabrina glanced over to the driver and found him dozing for a third time, only this time his foot was still pushing down on the accelerator and the cab was picking up speed. Instinctively, Sabrina grabbed the wheel, though she didn't have a clue how to drive a car.

"Help!" she cried. "He's out cold again!"

Granny reached forward and pushed hard on the horn, and the man nearly jumped out of his seat. "Wowie-kazowie!" he exclaimed, giving the steering wheel a quick turn that sent the cab careening into a parking lot. He braked just inches away from a dump truck. Everyone sat still and caught their breaths. As they calmed themselves, the dump truck started up, then pulled away, revealing a shocking sight behind it.

The ruins of the old school were completely gone, and in its place stood a brand-new building. Workers wearing bright orange hard hats hustled from one place to the next, nailing the last details into place.

"It's impossible," Sabrina said as she opened her door and stepped out of the cab. How could a brand-new school have been built in such a short time? She knew the answer the second she spotted the Three, a trio of witches: Morgan le Fay, Glinda the Good Witch, and Frau Pfefferkuchenhaus, the sorceress from the Hansel and Gretel story. They worked for Mayor Charming, making the impossible possible and cleaning up more than a few messes in the dark of night. Now they were zipping around overhead, inspecting their creation.

The whole scene made Sabrina sick to her stomach. Mr. Canis was buried beneath the new school. He had died saving the children of Ferryport Landing, and this was how the town repaid him? If Sabrina could have, she would have ripped the new school down with her bare hands rather than have her grandmother see it.

"We should go," Sabrina said as she turned to Granny Relda. "This town is heartless."

"I'll be all right, *liebling*," Granny said, then turned to the driver. "I'd appreciate you waiting. We're going to leave Elvis here with you."

"No way, lady!" Mr. Van Winkle said as Elvis licked his face. "This thing is a menace on four legs."

"But just imagine the tip you'll get if you stick around," Granny said.

The driver scowled but nodded his head. "Make it quick, will ya?"

The family got out of the car and buttoned their coats to fight the bitter chill.

"Hello, Mrs. Grimm," Morgan le Fay said, sashaying over to the group. She was a beautiful woman, and the construction workers ogled her every move. "Isn't it wonderful?"

"Yes, for a grave," Sabrina replied.

Morgan's smile disappeared. "Yes, I heard about what happened. My thoughts are with you and your girls, Relda. Mr. Canis was a good man. Well, I won't keep you. It's cold out here," she said, as she handed each of them a button with VOTE FOR CHARMING! printed on it in big purple letters.

Granny Relda thanked the woman, then led the children into the building, where they found a series of paper signs pointing in the direction of the celebration. The signs ended at two double doors, which Granny pushed open so the group could step into the school's new gymnasium.

The sounds of merriment filled Sabrina's ears. Every Everafter she had met since arriving in Ferryport Landing, and a whole bunch she had never seen before, stood around talking. A round little robot man made entirely of copper stood nearby talking to a skinny man with an enormous pumpkin for a head. A black panther and a huge gray bear talked politics in a corner. There were ogres, witches, fairy godmothers, an occasional cyclops, an enormous caterpillar smoking a hookah pipe, and dozens and dozens of handsome princes and beautiful princesses gathered in small clusters. A beautiful brown-skinned woman in a green dress smiled and waved at Granny Relda.

"It's nice to see you, Briar Rose," Granny called out to her.

"Who's that?" Daphne asked.

"You know her better as Sleeping Beauty," the old woman said.

Daphne opened her mouth, inserted her palm, and bit down.

"What are you doing here?" a voice asked from behind them. Sabrina spun around and found a very small man in a black suit eyeing them disapprovingly. Mr. Seven, as he was known, was the mayor's assistant, limo driver, and personal whipping boy. He was also one of the seven dwarfs. He looked nervous, sweaty, and exhausted.

"Hello, Mr. Seven. Snow White invited us down to see the new school," Granny Relda said to the little man.

"Well, you've seen it. It's great, isn't it? Now why don't you leave? The boss is going to blow his top if he finds you here. He's in a foul mood today," the little man said, looking around nervously.

"You mean worse than his normal foul mood?" Sabrina asked.

Just then a tall, broad-shouldered man in a purple suit swaggered into the gym. He was impossibly handsome, with dazzling blue eyes, a strong jaw, and perfectly combed black hair. His face was one big smile, and he shook hands with everyone he encountered. He came over and grabbed Sabrina's good hand without even looking at her. He shook it vigorously, then peered at her closely. He yanked the wool scarf from her face and groaned.

"Mr. Seven, what are the Grimms doing here?" Mayor Charming demanded.

The little man fumbled for words but had no answer.

Mayor Charming was the hero of about a dozen fairy tales. Also known as Prince Charming, he had saved many a damsel in distress—and married a good number of them, too—but somewhere along the way he'd stopped being charming and turned into a first-class jerk. He was rude and condescending, and for almost two hundred years he had been in a bitter feud with Sabrina's family. He vowed to some-day buy up the whole town and knock down the Grimm house. Still, there was more to him than just nasty hot air. Sabrina had to admit that the mayor came through in a pinch—once lending a hand to stop a giant from destroying the town, then helping to prevent Rum-pelstiltskin from breaking through the magical barrier that kept the Everafters trapped in Ferryport Landing—but Sabrina wondered if his rare moments of heroics didn't serve some other selfish purpose.

"Mr. Seven, I asked you a question. Who was the moron who invited the Grimms?" Charming asked angrily.

"I invited them."

Charming spun around and found Snow White entering the gym-nasium. At one time the mayor and the teacher had been engaged to be married, but Snow White left the prince at the altar, putting an end to their "happily ever after." Sabrina couldn't blame her. Sure, Charm-ing was nice to look at, but when he opened his mouth, ugh! Still, it was obvious to anyone that the two were still in love with each other.

"When I said moron, I didn't mean you, of course," Charming stammered.

"I would hope not," Ms. White said.

"But, Snow, why on earth would you invite them?" the mayor asked. "This is a ceremony for the Everafter community. Almost everyone here hates this family."

"Well, I don't, Billy," Ms. White replied.

"Well, uh . . . ," Charming stammered. "Of course they're welcome."

He bent over and whispered in Sabrina's ear, "Take your grandmother and sister and find a rock to crawl under until this is over. And go wash your face, child. You look deranged.

"Well, I suppose it's showtime," he said, straightening up and forcing a smile to his face. "Don't want to keep the public waiting."

"Good luck," the beautiful teacher said. She stood on tippy-toes and kissed him on the cheek.

Charming's face turned bright red, and he looked a little dizzy. He mumbled a few incoherent words, then walked away.

"You've got quite a power over him," Mr. Seven said to Snow White, who blushed and giggled. "I wish we could have you around twenty-four hours a day."

She grinned. "If you'll excuse me, I'm going to find a spot a little closer to the stage."

Granny winked, and Snow White disappeared into the crowd.

Suddenly, two tubby men came through the double doors, followed by Sheriff Hamstead, a Grimm family friend. The two men wore white shirts, blue jeans, and hard hats, and they were carrying rolls of blueprints under their arms. Sabrina recognized them as the sheriff's former deputies, Boarman and Swineheart. To the casual observer the three looked like normal, everyday people, but Sabrina and her family knew their secret identities. Boarman, Swineheart, and Hamstead were really the Three Little Pigs in magical disguises. Hamstead was doing his best to get their attention, but they were both ignoring him.

"I can't believe you two won't even consider it," Hamstead complained.

"Listen, Ernest," Swineheart said, spinning around to face his former boss. "There's a reason we didn't invite you to be a partner in our construction company. You're obsessed with straw. This new school is made entirely out of wood and brick!"

"I'm just saying, straw has come a long way," Hamstead said. "It has all kinds of practical applications. It's the building material of the future."

"I'd agree if we were building something that was *supposed* to blow away," Boarman said. "A kite, for instance, would be perfect. But we're building a school, and one that sits very close to a river, too. One thunderstorm with twenty-mile-an-hour winds would knock a straw building over just like that."

The two rotund men walked away, leaving Hamstead to chase after them.

Mayor Charming climbed onto the stage and took his place at the podium. He tapped on the microphone and smiled widely. "Fine citizens of Ferryport Landing, welcome to a new era in our town's education."

"I don't know why everyone is celebrating," Puck said loudly. "Opening a new school is a depressing event."

The entire audience turned to look at the boy fairy.

"What? I'm really sad," he said defensively.

The mayor bit down on his lip to control his anger before he continued.

"I'd like to thank some of the community organizations that have made this event possible. First, let's hear a round of applause for our co-sponsors and the hosts of today's celebration—Fairy Godmothers Against Drunk Driving."

Several blue-haired ladies in fluffy dresses floated into the air, held aloft by the flapping wings on their backs. They all wore T-shirts with the letters FGMADD on them. The crowd applauded.

"I also want to thank the League of Wiccan Voters, the National Association for the Advancement of Handsome Princes, Big Brothers and Ugly Stepsisters of America, and Everafters for the Ethical Treatment of Talking Animals. Their hard work and dedication to this important project has been vital to its success."

The crowd applauded again.

"When Ferryport Landing Elementary was destroyed three days ago, I came out to this site, and do you know what I heard?"

There was a brief silence and then a loud, squeaky fart. Sabrina turned and saw Puck fall over with laughter. For once, one of his childish pranks was well timed. *Ruin Charming's stupid little event!* Sabrina secretly cheered. *I'm starting to enjoy evil Puck!*

"I heard the future calling," Charming said angrily. He regained his composure and continued. "And I saw an opportunity for our children. When I talk about our children, I don't mean the children of everyone in this town. I'm talking about Everafter children, who for many years have been denied instruction in our community's rich traditions and history. They have been pushed into the shadows when it comes to their unique needs, for fear of drawing the attention of their human classmates. For far too long, there has been no room for them at the head of the class. What we have built here together represents a new day for them."

The crowd roared with approval.

"I have personally overseen this project—supervising the work, even rolling up my sleeves and picking up a shovel to help out," Charming said, causing some in the audience to laugh good-naturedly. "Boarman and Swineheart Construction has done an amazing job."

"It's Swineheart and Boarman Construction!" Swineheart shouted.

"No, it's not. It's Boarman and Swineheart Construction," his partner argued.

Charming cleared his throat, and the bickering ended.

"And we couldn't have done any of this without generous donations from our town's three wealthiest families. Everyone give a round of applause to Little Miss Muffet and the spider—I mean, Mr. and Mrs. Harry Arachnid—and to Beauty and the Beast, and, of course, to the Frog Prince and his lovely princess."

The three couples stood off to the side, obviously fuming but doing their best to hide it. They waved halfheartedly to the crowd. Only a few days earlier, the Grimms had discovered that these "wealthy donors" had gotten rich selling their Everafter children to Rumpelstiltskin. Sabrina was sure their "generous donations" were little more than bribes to keep them out of prison.

"Some people asked me, 'Mayor Charming, what's the big deal? There are only a few Everafter children in this town. Why make all the fuss?' Well, I'll tell you why I'm making a fuss. Because you people elected me to make a fuss!"

He was again met with wild applause.

"The new school will have separate, exclusive classes for Everafter children. It will feature a cafeteria offering lunches that meet the special dietary needs of our unique offspring. And lastly, it will be named after one of our own. From this day forward, the children of Ferryport Landing, whether human or Everafter, will learn in a school named after one of the most respected Everafters in our community. Ladies and gentlemen, I proudly present to you Ferryport Landing's answer to the call of the future . . ."

Mr. Seven tugged on a large curtain behind the mayor. It fell to the floor, revealing a banner that read WILLIAM CHARMING ELEMENTARY. Below it was a huge bronze statue of the mayor standing with his chest puffed out and a wide grin on his face. Several frightened-looking children crouched at his feet, gazing up at him as if he were their only hope for survival.

The room was silent; then the grumbling began. Only Mr. Seven clapped, and he did it desperately, as if he feared for his job.

Suddenly, Sabrina was shoved from behind. A group of people forced their way through the crowd and up to the podium. Their leader was a chubby woman wearing a long red dress and a golden crown. Her face was covered in white powder, and a little black birthmark had been drawn on her cheek. Beside her was a small army of men in colorful uniforms. When Sabrina examined them more closely, she was shocked to discover their bodies were actually playing cards. The woman climbed up on the stage and snatched the microphone out of the mayor's hand. The Queen of Hearts had arrived.

"I don't see any cause to celebrate," the queen said. "Having to rebuild this school is an unacceptable waste of taxpayer money, and you, Mayor Charming, are to blame!"

Charming was startled but quickly recovered, then smiled widely at the irate woman. "Mrs. Heart, so glad you could attend our little party. Your support for causes like this is essential. However, we're not here to debate politics—we're here to dedicate this wonderful new school to the youth of this town."

Mr. Seven clapped again, alone.

"The school wouldn't have had to be rebuilt if it weren't for you," the queen said as she turned to the crowd. "Everafters of Ferryport Landing, this sorry excuse for a mayor has let us down once again. In the last month, we've had a giant run amok, causing property damage in the millions. Our police force has been reduced to one pig, and public services, utilities, and infrastructure are falling by the wayside. Three days ago, a perfectly good elementary school was blown to smithereens, and you are footing the bill. Charming is completely incompetent."

"What's *incompetent* mean?" Daphne asked.

"It means he's not good at his job," Sabrina replied.

"The town has been in a bit of a budget crisis of late," the mayor said, looking defensive. "I have done the best I could with the resources at hand. But as you know, I'm the mayor of both our community and the humans. The money has to be equally divided."

"Is that good enough for us?" the queen cried.

Several people in the audience grumbled. A few even shouted, "No!"

"No, it's not good enough!" the queen shouted. "And worse, you don't know how truly bad things have gotten. Mayor Charming deputized the Grimms!"

A gasp rolled through the crowd.

"That's a bit of an exaggeration," Charming said, smiling through gritted teeth.

"So, you didn't hire the Grimms to help Hamstead investigate crimes?"

"Well, yes, I did," the mayor replied, as another gasp ran through the audience. "We were having an emergency. Rumpelstiltskin was going to . . . he built tunnels . . . the Grimms have special talents . . ." Charming was obviously rattled.

"So, now the only people who can solve Everafter problems are humans? You heard it yourself, folks. Your elected leader thinks that we can't govern ourselves, that we need help from humans—and not just any humans," the queen raged, "but the family that is responsible for our imprisonment!" She turned and pointed an ugly finger right at Granny Relda and the girls. "The Grimms!"

Sabrina gasped. Never had she felt so much rage aimed at her and her family. She'd gotten used to knowing that many people in the town disliked them, but the queen's anger was rabid, and worse, it was infecting the crowd. Everywhere she looked, furious eyes stared back at them. Instinctively, she stepped forward, putting herself between the crowd and her family.

"Mrs. Heart, I won't have you stand up here and tell this crowd that I'm a fan of the Grimms," Charming said. "No one despises that family more than I do!"

"Hey!" Daphne shouted. "We can hear you, ya know!"

The queen continued her rant. "Who knows how much influence Relda and her brood have over the mayor's office? Are they making our laws, too? I think it's time for a change. I think it's time for new leadership! Today I'm announcing my candidacy for mayor of Ferryport Landing!" the Queen of Hearts declared. "And let me introduce you to the man who will become Ferryport Landing's new sheriff once I'm elected. He's a man of integrity—a man with centuries of experience—a man with a *legitimate* and *respected* career in law enforcement. Ladies and gentleman, Sheriff Nottingham!"

A tall, broad-shouldered man with a handlebar mustache and long curly black hair climbed to the stage. Despite a profound limp in his right leg, he was all aggression, from the deadly sneer on his lips to the lengthy scar on his cheek to the clenched fists at his side. He looked at the crowd, unable to hide his disgust with all of them, but then forced an insincere smile to his face.

Several people cheered.

"Maybe we should go," Granny Relda said to the girls.

"I agree," someone said. "Why are you even here? This celebration is for Everafters." The family spun around and saw a large group of Munchkins gathered nearby. Their leader's eyes flared with rage.

"I have as much right to be here as you do," Granny Relda

replied tartly. "My family has been here as long as any Ever-after."

"It'ssss your fault we're trapped here in thissss town," an enormous boa constrictor said as it slithered along the floor toward the Grimms.

An old witch hobbled toward them, pointing her gnarled finger at the family. "Charming has been giving your family a free ride for far too long. Heart is right—it's time for a change."

A small crowd of beasties, hobgoblins, and elves formed a tight circle around the family, cutting off their escape. "We've had enough!" a crow as big as a dog squawked. "The only thing that has kept you safe until now is the Big Bad Wolf. Now that your mongrel is dead and gone, what will you do?"

Daphne grabbed Puck's arm. "Do something!"

"Sorry, marshmallow. I told you, I'm back to being sinister."

"Well, if we get killed, you'll have no one to annoy all day long."

The boy heaved an exasperated sigh and nodded his head. He spread his wings and drew his sword.

"Back off, you filthy trash muncher!" he said to the crow. "The Grimms are mine to torment. Take another step, and you'll be wishing the Wolf were still alive."

A cyclops stepped forward and cracked his knuckles. "Boy, I will pound you into pudding."

"Whatever!" Puck said as his arms morphed into a gorilla's. He pulled back and hit the cyclops right in the belly, sending him flying backward. The monster knocked Everafters over like bowling pins.

"Who's next?" the boy crowed. "Who thinks they can take on the Trickster King?"

A small angry old man answered the challenge. His body grew. His clothing ripped, exposing a sickening green skin underneath. His cane morphed into an ugly, blood-smeared club nearly as big as the cyclops Puck had just flattened. He was a troll, the largest one Sabrina had ever seen. Worse, he was the angriest one she'd ever seen.

Everafters scattered in all directions as he stepped toward the family.

"Come here, meat!" he growled.

"You are about to suffer one of the worst beatings of your life, ugly," Puck said without flinching. "The Prince of Fairies isn't some billy goat you can scare off a bridge."

Puck swung his sword and smacked the troll in the belly, to little effect. The monster looked more annoyed than hurt. With lightning-fast reflexes, the brute lunged forward and knocked Puck to the ground, then sat hunched over the boy, flashing his horrible, drool-dripping teeth. His neck muscles clenched as he prepared to feast on the boy. But suddenly there was a popping sound, and Sabrina looked up to see a man materialize from thin air high above the gymnasium floor. He fell hard and fast, landing on top of the troll's back. The creature grunted with surprise, then bucked and kicked as he tried to remove his unwanted passenger. The strange man held on for dear life. He reached into his overcoat and removed a small ring he then slipped onto his finger. He uttered a few unintelligible words, and a cloud of black smoke swirled around the monster's head, blinding him.

"That's just about enough! Now, calm down, Howard, or I'm going to get rough!" the stranger shouted.

The troll stumbled around, unable to see. He knocked over the statue of Charming, and it fell to the ground. The head broke off and rolled across the floor until it stopped at Sabrina's feet. His smug face looked up into hers.

"Get off of me, flea!" the troll cried.

"Are you going to be a good boy?" the stranger demanded.

The troll fought for several more minutes before surrendering. "Yes!"

Satisfied, the stranger put his ring away, and the cloud of smoke evaporated into nothing.

"Now go home and stay there until you've learned some manners," he said to the hulking figure. "What would your wife think of your behavior?"

The troll lowered his eyes in shame and, along with several other Everafters, exited the gymnasium.

Daphne grabbed Sabrina's hand. "That's the man from last night!" she whispered.

Sabrina eyed the stranger closely. Her sister was right. The weirdo who had attacked them the night before had just saved their lives.

He rushed to the family and took Granny Relda into his arms. Sabrina watched dumbfounded as he gave the old woman a huge hug and a kiss on the cheek.

"Are you OK, Mom?"

"Mom?" Sabrina, Daphne, and Puck cried at the same time.

"I'm fine, Jacob," Granny replied.

5

THE MAN HUGGED GRANNY RELDA TIGHTLY AND lifted her off her feet.

"Jacob, put me down." She laughed. "I'm an old woman."

The man set her back down. "You're not so old," he said.

"You look so thin! And what happened to your nose?"

The man shuffled his feet like a schoolboy who'd been caught placing a tack on his teacher's seat.

"It was nothing—just a little misunderstanding with a frost giant in Nepal. I think it makes me look rugged."

Puck stepped between the two and shoved his sword under the man's chin. "Step away from the old lady, or I'll run you through."

"Puck, this is my son," Granny said, pulling the boy away.

"Your son!" the girls cried.

"Yes—your uncle Jacob," the old woman said.

"Call me Uncle Jake," said the man, opening his arms for a hug the girls didn't deliver. Sabrina was too stunned. For the second time in less than two months, the sisters were being introduced to a family member they hadn't known existed.

"Henry didn't tell them about me?" the man asked, seeming to read the girls' minds.

"Henry didn't tell them about me, either," Granny Relda said.

"Well, I'm happy to finally meet you," said the man with a wink that told them he knew the previous night's encounter was a secret.

"You must be Daphne," he said. "You've got Hank's grin."

"Hank?" Daphne asked.

"That's what we used to call your dad when he was a kid," Uncle Jake said turning to Sabrina. "And that means you're Sabrina. I am curious: Is the mustache and goatee some kind of fad I am unaware of, or did you lose a bet?"

Sabrina scowled and pulled her scarf back up to her nose.

"And this is Puck," Granny said.

"I didn't need your help," Puck grunted at Uncle Jake before he could say hello. "I had everything under control."

Uncle Jake laughed. "Listen, kid, you were knee-deep in trouble, and you know it."

"*Boys!*" Granny said. "Play nice."

Puck's face crinkled like he smelled a rotten egg. He huffed and shoved his sword back into his belt, then turned toward the exit.

"Where are you going?" Granny Relda asked.

"Away!" the boy snapped as he kicked the doors open. Before anyone could stop him, he was gone.

Sheriff Hamstead hobbled over to the group. His overworked belt had broken during the melee, and he was having a terrible time keeping his pants up. "Relda, are you and the children OK?"

"Yes, yes, just a little shaken up. Was anyone hurt?"

"Not seriously," Hamstead answered as he looked around to be sure. "I've gotten the mayor, Mr. Seven, and Ms. White to safety, and I'm asking everyone to go home."

"Of course," Granny Relda said.

"Hamstead! How are you doing? It's been a long time," Uncle Jake said, hugging the policeman. Sabrina looked over at her sister. Apparently the "hugging thing" that Daphne was always doing ran in the family. Uncle Jake squeezed the man so tightly, Hamstead was unable to stop his pants from slipping down to his ankles, revealing boxer shorts with little pink cupids on them.

"Uh . . . do I know you, mister?" the sheriff asked, with his face squished against Jake's chest.

Uncle Jake stepped back in surprise. "Know me? Of course you know me."

"Sheriff, this is my son Jacob," Granny Relda said.

Hamstead quickly pulled up his pants. "Relda, I didn't know you had another son," he said.

"Ernest, what are you talking about?" Uncle Jake asked. "You don't remember my brother and me? You caught us cutting school all the time. You took Hank and me down to the jail and locked us in a cell once. You told us that kids who skipped class had to go to prison and break rocks. It scared us half to death. We never cut again."

The sheriff studied Uncle Jake's face closely, but it was obvious to anyone that he didn't recognize the man. "Sorry, son. I chase down a lot of truants."

"But—"

Granny took her son by the sleeve and pulled him toward the exit before he could finish his sentence. "Let us know if you need any help, Sheriff."

She hustled the family outside and across the parking lot, where they found Mr. Van Winkle sound asleep in his cab. Elvis was in the front seat and was also snoring happily with his head resting on the old man's lap. The sack with the mozzarella-and-pepper sandwich had been torn open and its contents consumed. When Elvis let out a rather loud burp, Sabrina knew it wouldn't take a detective to figure out who had stolen the cab driver's lunch.

"You're not still using cars to get around, are you?" Uncle Jake asked. "Why not use a flying carpet or something in the teleportation room? Mirror has all kinds of stuff!"

"I prefer to do some things the old-fashioned way," Granny said.

Uncle Jake rolled his eyes. "More like prehistoric."

Granny Relda opened the car door and tapped the horn. The cabbie jumped in his seat. "Sweet mother of pearl!" he shouted. "What? Is it over?"

"We're ready to go."

Mr. Van Winkle rubbed his tired eyes and looked down at Elvis. Then he noticed the remains of his lunch.

"Your dog is a menace," he complained.

The big dog licked his lips with an expression that seemed to say, *Who, me?*

"Elvis, that's not very nice," Granny said. "We'll stop on the way home and get you something to eat, Mr. Van Winkle."

"And a cup of coffee," Sabrina grumbled as she climbed into the front seat next to the gassy dog.

By the time Mr. Van Winkle pulled the cab into the driveway of the family's two-story yellow house, everyone was a nervous wreck. Granny shoved a handful of bills into the cabbie's hands.

"Thanks for the ride," the old woman said. "And happy holidays to you."

Mr. Van Winkle seemed pleased with his tip. "Sure, lady. And remember: The next time you need fast, reliable, and friendly service, call me," he said as he shoved business cards into everyone's hands. "But next time the fur ball stays home."

Moments later he was gone. "This place hasn't changed at all," Uncle Jake said as he marveled at the little house. "I bet there's still a dozen Frisbees on the roof."

"Things don't change much in Ferryport Landing," Granny said as she climbed the porch steps to the front door.

"Wait a minute! I know something that's different. Why isn't the house decorated for the holidays?"

The old woman blushed as if she was ashamed.

"When we were kids, this place had so many lights on it you could probably see it from space," Uncle Jake told the girls. "The electric bill was so thick they had to spiral-bind it."

"We've been a bit busy lately," Granny Relda explained.

"Well, leave the decorating to me, then," her son said as he reached into his pocket and took out a long, carved wand. "I'll have this place looking like the North Pole in no time."

"Jake, I absolutely forbid it," Granny Relda said, but Uncle Jake ignored her.

He held the wand aloft and shouted, "Gimme some Christmas!"

Blinding rays of red and green light illuminated the yard. Within the beams Sabrina could see tiny particles moving and rearranging into solid objects that zipped across the lawn and grew in size. Suddenly, two enormous inflatable snowmen appeared in the center of the yard. A row of ten-foot-tall candy canes lined the driveway all the way to the end. Red ribbons encircled the porch banisters, and a mechanical Santa Claus in a shiny sleigh landed on top of the house. An odd, robotic "Ho, Ho, Ho!" blasted out of its mouth. Lines of multicolored blinking lights encircled every tree, bush, and shrub. Even poor Elvis found himself wrapped from head to toe in twinkling lights.

"That takes care of the outside," he said, marching up the steps to the front door.

Daphne ran to a candy cane, sniffed it, then gave it a lick. "Hey! This is real!"

"Let it be, Daphne. You'll spoil your dinner," the old woman said as she went to work unlocking the door.

"C'mon, Mom, let them have some fun." He handed the wand to Sabrina. "Want to give it a try?"

The moment it touched her fingers, Sabrina felt a charge race through her like nothing she had ever felt. It went all the way down to her toes then shot back up to the top of her head.

"What do I do?" she asked, as the family filed into the house.

"Imagine how you want everything to look," Uncle Jake said. "And then ask for it.'"

"Jake, I don't think this is an appropriate exercise for the girls," Granny scolded.

Sabrina aimed the wand at the living room.

"Sabrina Grimm, I absolutely forbid it!" Granny cried, but she was too late.

"Gimme some Christmas," Sabrina said, and light blasted out of the wand. The rearranging particles twisted and turned, then eventually became a beautiful white-needled tree, covered in shiny bulbs and lights, showered in tinsel, strung with popcorn garlands, and topped with a porcelain angel. Mountains of presents were tucked underneath. A choo-choo train raced around the room on a track, and Bing Crosby crooned "White Christmas" from a stereo exactly like the one Sabrina and Daphne's parents had once owned in New York City.

"Wow!" Daphne cried.

Granny raced over to Sabrina and snatched the wand out of her hand. The little charge vanished, and Sabrina immediately wished she could get it back.

"Jacob Alexander Grimm! I said no!"

"Oh, Mom, don't be a humbug," Uncle Jake said. "It's the girls' first Christmas in the house. It should be memorable."

"I wholeheartedly agree, but I don't think we need magic to do that," Granny said as she put the wand back in her son's hand. "One of the special things about Christmas is that the family decorates the house together."

"Says you! Why do something in days when you can do it in seconds?"

Granny shook her head. It was clear she disapproved of Uncle Jake's attitude.

The morning slipped into afternoon and finally into evening as Uncle Jake told one hair-raising story after another about his many adventures. The girls hung on his every word; even Granny was fascinated with her son's tales and eventually decided to order pizza for dinner rather than miss a single word while she was cooking.

"So how come we've never met you before?" Daphne asked as she helped herself to another pepperoni slice.

"Well, I've been traveling the world and getting into trouble," Uncle Jake said with a grin. "For a while I lived in Prague with Tom Thumb, and then I spent some time in India, Russia, Japan, Germany, and even Costa Rica, but lately I've been working with the Andersen Triplets."

"Who are they?" Sabrina said.

"You don't know who the Andersen Triplets are?" Uncle Jake said in a way that made Sabrina feel self-conscious.

"Henry chose to keep the children out of the loop when it came to the family business," Granny Relda said.

"All of it?"

The old woman nodded. "Unfortunately, we've been a little busy around here, so there hasn't been time to explain everything."

"Where do I start?" Uncle Jake said. "OK, you two are the Sisters Grimm because you are descendants of the Brothers Grimm. The Andersen Triplets are the descendants of Hans Christian Andersen."

"So they're fairy-tale detectives, too?" asked Daphne.

"Not at all. They're magic hunters. They track down and collect enchanted items," Uncle Jake said as he retrieved the wand from his pocket. "That's how I got this bad boy. It's Merlin's wand, straight from Camelot. The Triplets found it at a garage sale in Athens, Ohio. The owner thought it was a back scratcher. Mom, you wouldn't believe the stuff they've got in storage. It rivals the Hall of Wonders."

Granny frowned. "Which explains how you suddenly appeared out of thin air."

Uncle Jake grinned. He stood up, removed a jewel-encrusted belt from around his waist, and placed it on the table.

"The Nome King's belt?" Granny asked.

"One of my first finds," Jack said, proudly. "Though I think the batteries are dying. I wanted to pop in right next to the troll, but this thing put me ten feet above him."

"Who's the Nome King?" Daphne asked.

"You've never heard of the Nome King?"

"Henry forbid them from reading fairy tales, too," Granny Relda explained.

"He what? That's crazy. OK, the Nome King is from Oz. He

was in one of Baum's histories—*Ozma of Oz*, if I'm correct. The Nome King was the ruler of an underground kingdom, underneath a land called Ev that was across the desert from Oz. I hear it's all condos and golf courses now. Anyway, Dorothy Gale washed up on the beach there after she fell out of a boat."

"Dorothy is a little accident prone," Granny said, rolling her eyes.

"If you tell me Dorothy lives in Ferryport Landing, I'm going to freak out!" Daphne cried.

"No, a sleepy little place like this wasn't exciting enough for Ms. Gale. I met her about a year ago. She's a tornado chaser for some science institute, collecting data on storms, but personally I think she does it for the adrenaline rush. She's got nerves of steel. Anyway, Dorothy managed to get the belt away from the little man, and it helped her get back to Kansas. It works just like the magic slippers. Imagine yourself somewhere and—bingo-bango!—you're there!"

"And it runs on batteries?" Sabrina asked, not quite sure if her uncle was pulling her leg.

"Yeah, twelve of the big ones, and they get drained pretty fast. It costs me almost thirty bucks every time I use this thing—even if it's just to pop up across the street."

"You could always walk," Granny muttered.

"You haven't changed a bit, have you?" Uncle Jake said with a laugh. "Still anti-magic?"

"I'm not anti-magic. I just think it makes people lazy, and it can be very addictive. Before some people know it, all they can think about is magic rings and wands and flying carpets."

"That reminds me of a funny story. Once Hank and I got the magic carpet out, and—"

"Why don't we use the belt to find Mom and Dad?" Sabrina interrupted.

"Sorry, 'Brina," Uncle Jake said. "You have to know an exact location. But don't worry—Jake Grimm is on the case. We're going to get your parents home in no time. That's why I came back to town."

Sabrina grinned from ear to ear. Finally, there was someone in this family besides herself dedicated to bringing her mom and dad home. She felt a tremendous weight lift off her shoulders. Now she had help.

"It's getting late, and the girls need their rest," Granny said. "We can take more of this trip down memory lane in the morning."

"What about Puck?" Daphne asked, tossing a slice of pizza into the air for Elvis to catch in his hungry jaws.

"He'll be back when he's ready. The boy has slept outside most of his life. He'll be fine," the old woman assured them. "Jacob, I'll get some blankets and a pillow for you. You can sleep on the couch tonight."

"Why can't I sleep in my own room?" Uncle Jake complained.

"It's not your room anymore," the old woman said. "I gave it to Mirror after you left."

"You gave my room to the magic mirror?" Jake cried. "He doesn't need his own room. You could put him in a closet."

"That would be a little rude. You'll be fine on the couch. Come along, *lieblings*," the old woman said, ignoring her son's protests.

The girls climbed the stairs to bed, stopping in the bathroom to wash their faces and hands and brush their teeth. Daphne slipped into her favorite pair of footy pajamas, then helped Sabrina put on an old T-shirt and flannel pajama bottoms. The sisters crawled into bed.

"Can you believe we have an uncle?" Daphne asked.

"I can believe just about anything with this family," Sabrina answered. "I wonder why Dad never told us about him."

"I guess he was trying to protect us from all of this, but . . ."

"But what?"

Daphne pointed at a photo hanging on the wall. In it, two boys sat on a steep hill overlooking the Hudson River. Sabrina knew one of the boys was her father. She'd always assumed the other was a childhood friend. Looking closely at the second boy, she saw the now familiar quirky grin. "Well, there's only this one picture of Uncle Jake in the whole house."

"So?"

"So that's not how a mom acts," Daphne said. "Think about all the pictures Mom took of us. They were all over the apartment. Since we moved here, Granny's taken at least a million more. There are pictures of Mom and Dad, Grandpa, and Mr. Canis all over the place. There are three dozen of Elvis in the living room alone. Why not Uncle Jake?"

"That is a little odd," Sabrina said.

"And why isn't there a journal for Uncle Jake on the shelves? It seems like Granny was trying to hide him from us," Daphne said. "She went to a lot of trouble to make it seem like he was never born."

A tap on the window woke Sabrina. Unsure if she had imagined it, she lay in bed until she heard it again. *Puck! He lost his keys and needs me to let him in the house.* She climbed out from under her blankets and went to the window. When she peered out, she saw her father and mother standing in the yard below. Sabrina tried to open the window but couldn't, quickly remembering that Mr. Canis had nailed it shut for their protection shortly after the girls arrived.

"Daphne! Wake up!" Sabrina shouted, but the little girl was sound asleep. From past experience, Sabrina knew that sometimes her sister was impossible to wake, so she raced out of the room alone.

Down the stairs she went, two at a time. Without bothering to put on shoes or a coat, she darted out the front door and around to the side of the house.

"Mom! Dad!" she cried, as she turned the corner and ran smack into something enormous. She fell to the cold ground and looked up. The Jabberwocky was standing over her. On each of its disgusting hands was a puppet, one sewn to resemble a man with blond hair and the other a woman with raven locks, crudely similar to her parents. Sitting on the beast's shoulders was Little Red Riding Hood.

Sabrina crawled backward across the frozen grass, desperate to get away, but the monster was too fast. It tossed its puppets aside, reached down, and snatched Sabrina off the ground. It pulled her close to its thousand gnashing teeth while Red Riding Hood leaned down and smiled as if they were great friends.

"Want to play house?" the little girl asked in her singsong voice.

That was when Sabrina woke up. Her pajamas were soaked with sweat, and her head was pounding. She looked around the bedroom to double-check that she was indeed awake and fought the urge to cry.

She awkwardly crawled out of bed and tiptoed across the floor to the window. The backyard was empty, so she sat back down on the bed until she felt better. There would be no more sleeping this night, so she slipped into the hallway. She crept down the steps and into the living room, where her uncle slept on the couch. His overcoat, with its hundreds of pockets, was draped over the back. Sabrina knew that Little Red Riding Hood's medical file was in one of them. She could wait for her uncle to wake up, but time was wasting. She stepped softly to the couch and lifted the long coat. She quickly found the file, but before she could grab it and hurry back upstairs, Uncle Jake's hand seized her arm.

"You're good," he said. "But you missed the creaky beam on the bottom step. I could never get around that. Your grandmother caught your father and me more times than I can count because of that last step."

Sabrina tried to pull away from his grasp, but he held on.

"You could have just asked for it," he continued. Her uncle reached into his overcoat and removed Red Riding Hood's rolled-up medical file. He released Sabrina's arm and handed it to her.

"I'm sorry. I'm used to having to do everything in secret," Sabrina tried to explain. "Granny doesn't want us getting involved with Red Riding Hood. She says she's too dangerous. I figured you'd just say the same."

"I love my mom, but we rarely agree on anything," Uncle Jake said with a laugh. "But that doesn't mean she isn't right about Red. Red's dangerous. But we still have to face her to get Henry and Veronica home. I figure we can get both of them home a lot faster if we work together—you know, in secret."

Faster was what Sabrina wanted. She nodded, and Uncle Jake leaped off the couch. "Good, let's get started. But first we need a little magic." He led her into the kitchen and flipped on the light, then searched through every cabinet until he finally found what he wanted—a can of coffee. "Ah, liquid magic," he said with a grin.

Sabrina's mom and dad were coffee fanatics. They drank it morning, noon, and night. Her mother used to wait in long lines and pay more than five bucks for a cup of foam she called a latte. When her father was late for work, he'd take his mug with him into the shower.

Uncle Jake found some filters in a drawer and an ancient instruction manual for the coffeemaker. In no time, the smell of fresh roast was filling the room, and his magic potion was dripping into the pot. When the coffee was finished, he poured out two mugs' worth and handed one to Sabrina.

"Dad said it isn't good for a kid," Sabrina said. "He said it would stunt my growth."

"Sabrina, I'm six feet two inches tall. I think you'll be fine," Jake said, nudging the cup into her hands.

She took a sip. It was bitter and gross and tasted a lot like mud. She spat it out into the sink, turned on the faucet, and stuck her mouth under the cool water to wash out the taste.

"When you get older, you'll love it," her uncle said.

"If this is what I have to look forward to when I'm older, I think I'll stay eleven."

He opened the sugar bowl and spooned three heaping helpings into Sabrina's mug. "This will kill the bitterness."

Sabrina stirred the concoction and took another sip. It was better. He led her into the dining room, and they both sat down. Sabrina set Red Riding Hood's medical file on the table, and her uncle opened it.

"So, about the other night," Uncle Jake said. "You kids didn't give me much of a chance to explain who I was."

"We don't usually give the benefit of the doubt to weirdos hanging around in burnt-out buildings," Sabrina said.

"Takes one to know one." Uncle Jake laughed. "I looked through this earlier, but I didn't understand much of it. There's a lot of medical mumbo jumbo in here. But I have discovered one thing."

"What's that?"

"Little Red Riding Hood is a certifiable loony tune."

Sabrina frowned. "I could have told you that."

Uncle Jake grinned. "I also found this," he said, passing her a yellowed sheet with typing on it. "Red's medical history."

Sabrina looked closely at it. It read much like Red Riding Hood's famous fairy-tale story. She was sent into the woods by her mother to take her old grandmother some food. Along the way she met a horrible beast she described as a wolf. When she got to the house, she saw what she thought was her grandmother sitting in bed, but her grandmother had actually been killed and eaten by the wolf. The beast put on her grandmother's clothing to fool the child so he could eat her, too. Just before the wolf could kill Little Red Riding Hood, the child discovered the disguise and ran into the woods. There she found a woodcutter who helped her hunt the wolf. When they captured the wolf, they cut him open and shoved rocks into his belly. Then the woodcutter tossed the wolf's body into the river where it sank to the bottom. The man took the girl back to the village in hopes of returning her to her family, but her parents were never found. It was her doctors' belief that Red Riding Hood's mind was severely distressed by these events, causing her to experience a break with reality. Everything her doctors had tried to make her well failed.

"The Big Bad Wolf drove her insane," Sabrina said. She thought of Mr. Canis. The old man hadn't seemed capable of such savagery, but his alter ego, the Wolf, was pure evil. For a moment, Sabrina felt sorry for Red Riding Hood.

"That's what her doctors thought, too, but you don't need a medical degree to figure that out. All you have to do is look at these."

He handed her a stack of aging papers. Sabrina flipped through them, each as delicate as a fallen leaf. The first few were finger

paintings of a family. There was a mother and a father holding a baby, a kitten, a grandmother, and a ferocious-looking dog. As Sabrina flipped through them, she found that the colors the girl used were less and less varied. The paintings got darker and darker, until eventually they were entirely black and red. They made her feel queasy.

"That's her family," Uncle Jake said. "There are dozens more."

"She never got over what happened," Sabrina said.

"No, I don't think a person can get over something like that, which is why I can understand what she's trying to do now."

"What do you mean?"

"Red is collecting a new family to replace the one she lost. Your mother and father are part of her collection."

Sabrina felt her blood stop running in her veins. Red was ten times scarier now that Sabrina understood what she was thinking. "When I confronted her, she said something about having a baby brother."

"Exactly," Uncle Jake said, pointing to the baby in the paintings.

"She said something else," Sabrina went on. "She said, 'Tell grandma and the puppy I'll see them soon. Then we can all play house.'"

"Who do we know around here who is a grandma with a dog?" Sabrina nearly cried out. *Granny Relda!*

Uncle Jake took the paintings and put them back into the file. "It doesn't tell us where Red Riding Hood may have gone, but at least we know her plan. We're all going to have to be prepared to defend my mom if that girl and her freaky pet show up."

"I don't know what kind of help I'm going to be," Sabrina said as she gestured to her broken arm.

"Oh, I'll fix that in a jiffy," Uncle Jake said, heading into the living room. He returned with his overcoat, sat back down, and started rifling through the pockets.

"Where did I put it?" he mumbled to himself. He took out a bottle, but it wasn't what he was looking for, so he tossed it aside. Sabrina peered down at the label, which read: EVIL EYE DROPS. A small tube labeled CURSE-B-GONE, and then a tub of cream called WITCH HAZEL REPELLENT were also rejected.

"Here it is," Uncle Jake said, finally pulling out a small round tin and handing it to Sabrina. She glanced at the label. SATIN SURGEON'S SALVE—NOW WITH A LEMONY FRESH SCENT!

"What's Satin Surgeon's Salve?" Sabrina asked as she popped the lid off. Inside was an icky black ointment that smelled like backed-up sewage. It made her gag.

"Andrew Lang wrote about this in *The Olive Fairy Book*. The story goes that there was a princess who saved the life of the man she loved with this stuff. The rumor is she got it from Cupid himself."

"What's in it?" Sabrina asked as she pinched her nose.

"You don't want to know." Uncle Jake took the tin and dipped his fingers into the rancid glop, which he rubbed over Sabrina's hand. The vile stuff felt as bad as it smelled. Her head started spinning, and an odd sensation ran up and down her arm, as if someone had poured an icy-cold glass of water into her cast. After a few seconds, the tingling stopped. Unfortunately, the smell remained.

"Feel better?" Uncle Jake asked.

Sabrina wasn't sure. The constant, dull pain in her arm was gone. She tried to move her fingers and found they wiggled easily. Uncle Jake got up and went into the kitchen, where he opened a drawer and rummaged through it. When he returned, he was carrying a pair of heavy kitchen scissors.

"The proof is in the pudding," he said as he cut her plaster cast. In no time her arm was free.

Sabrina rolled her shoulder slowly. She quickly realized that she could move her arm in any direction she wanted. It felt fine. In fact, it felt better than it ever had.

"It worked!" she cried.

"Of course it worked. It's magic. I just can't understand why my mother wouldn't have done this for you already. Mirror's got rooms of this stuff. Haven't you and your sister come across the pharmacy in the Hall of Wonders yet?"

"I'm not allowed in the Hall of Wonders." Sabrina sighed.

"You're kidding."

"I swiped Granny's keys and made copies without her permission. I've been banned."

"Wait—you don't have your own set of keys?" Uncle Jake exclaimed. "How do you and Daphne learn about all the stuff inside?"

"We don't. Granny says we're not ready."

"Not ready! You're practically over the hill! C'mon." Uncle Jake grabbed her arm with one hand and his overcoat with the other and rushed up the stairs. Once they got to the landing, they stopped at the door to Mirror's room, which Granny Relda always kept locked. Uncle Jake searched his pockets and quickly found a set of keys as large and impressive as the old woman's.

"I don't know about this," Sabrina whispered as he unlocked the door. "She really doesn't want me in there. When she found out what I had done, she went ballistic."

"Yeah, she does that a lot," Uncle Jake said as he opened the door. The two stepped inside and closed the door behind them.

Just then, a blinding bolt of lightning struck inches from their feet, leaving a black smoldering spot on the hardwood floor. "*Who dares invade my sanctuary?*" a horrible voice bellowed. Sabrina jumped back as a menacing face appeared in the mirror hanging on the opposite wall. It was filled with anger and power as a thunderstorm raged behind it.

"That was a little close, don't you think?" Sabrina complained, walking right up to the mirror.

"Sabrina? I'm so sorry," the face said, softening. "I thought I was being attacked by a pirate. Hang on for a second."

The face vanished, and when it came back it was wearing a pair of glasses with smart tortoiseshell frames.

"Oh, I *am* being attacked by a pirate," Mirror said, eyeing the girl's black-marker goatee and mustache closely. "Would it be safe to say that Puck had something to do with this particular accessory?"

Sabrina nodded.

"He's just delightful, isn't he?" Mirror replied sarcastically.

"Do you have any magic that removes permanent marker?" Sabrina grumbled to her uncle.

"Mirror?" Jake asked.

Mirror turned and focused his eyes on Uncle Jake. A huge grin appeared on his face. "Well, look what the cat dragged in!" he cried.

Jake rushed forward and did something most people would think impossible—he stepped into the reflection and vanished. Sabrina wasn't surprised in the least, though. After all, the mirror was more than just a reflective surface. It was also a doorway, and she followed her uncle through it.

On the other side was an enormous, barrel-vaulted hallway that reminded her of Grand Central Terminal in New York City. The ceiling was held up by massive marble columns. Rows and rows of arched doorways lined both walls. Each led to a different room packed with magical and otherworldly items. Granny called it the world's largest walk-in closet. The man known as Mirror called it the Hall of Wonders, and it was where he lived.

Jake hugged the little man tightly, causing him to drop a small book he was carrying. "It's good to see you, Mirror."

"It's good to be seen," Mirror said.

"You're looking great," Uncle Jake said, finally releasing him.

"Well, I do what I can. I drink a lot of water, and of course my Pilates instructor has really helped."

Sabrina leaned down and picked up Mirror's book. It was a paperback collection of word games like crosswords and jumbles.

"What's this?" she asked.

"Oh, Relda got it for me at the supermarket. She said she thought it might help pass the time. I could just kill her—I'm addicted to it now. Next time you see her, tell her to get me some more of them," Mirror said, turning his attention back to Uncle Jake. "What's with the family reunion, Jakey?"

"Jabberwocky stuff," the younger man said gravely.

"Yes, I heard it was back," Mirror said before turning to Sabrina. "That thing should have been destroyed long ago. I hope you haven't come here looking for something that can kill it."

"Oh, no." Uncle Jake sniffed. "No, we're here because I've got a niece in desperate need of a little magical training."

"I smell trouble," Mirror warned.

"I think that's the salve," Sabrina replied. The noxious medicine was still making her feel nauseated.

"Mirror! Don't worry," Uncle Jake said flashing his quirky grin. He handed the little man his huge set of keys. "Let's start with some hats."

"As you wish," Mirror replied. He turned and led them down the hallway. Lining the walls were doors of all shapes and sizes. Some were made of metal, others of wood, and one looked as if it was made of ice. A little bronze plaque told Sabrina what was behind each door: POISONED SPINNING WHEELS, TREE SPRITES, CRYSTAL BALLS, LOVE POTIONS, ALL THE KING'S HORSES (which was right next to ALL THE KING'S MEN). The doors went on and on— the hallway seemed to go on forever. Sabrina wondered aloud what might be at the end.

"You're not ready for that, Sabrina," Mirror said, then turned his attention back to Jake. "Relda will not be pleased."

"Mom is just being stubborn. The girls need to know what's in these rooms. Dad made sure that Hank and I knew how to use this stuff, and it got us out of a lot of close calls."

"It also got you into a lot of close calls, as I remember it," Mirror said.

Uncle Jake ignored the comment and turned to Sabrina. "Your dad and I spent hours in here every day, learning how the wands worked, testing out the magic shoes, learning how to fight with the swords and armor, and memorizing the translation spells so we could speak with birds, fish, and forest animals. These rooms are filled with very useful stuff."

Mirror stopped at a door with a plaque that read HATS, HELMETS, BEANIES, ETC. He found the key for the lock and opened the door. He stepped inside and soon returned with a metal helmet that had small antlers mounted on each side.

"Good choice," Uncle Jake said. "The Midas Crown."

"What does it do?" Sabrina asked, as her uncle placed it on her head.

"It makes you strong. Try to pick me up," Uncle Jake said.

"But you're three times my size."

"Try it!"

Sabrina reached over and grabbed her uncle by the shirt and lifted with all her strength. It was more than she needed. Uncle Jake went flying into the air and plummeted back into Sabrina's arms. His landing was awkward, but he wasn't hurt.

"Oh man, am I going to have fun with this!" Sabrina cried as she felt the power of the helmet course through her limbs. It was just like the jolt she had gotten from Merlin's wand.

"Sabrina, wait for me in the hall," a voice said behind them.

Sabrina turned and saw Granny Relda. The old woman's face was red with anger. Daphne stood next to her with sleepy eyes and a confused expression.

"Busted," Uncle Jake whispered.

"Hey! Your arm is healed," Daphne said.

"I suppose you used magic," Granny said.

"It was silly to have her in pain," Uncle Jake said. "Why wait two months when it could be perfectly fine today?"

"And what is the cost of that, Jacob?"

"I don't understand the question."

"There is a cost with magic. There is always a cost."

"There's no cost. Her arm is healed," Uncle Jake said defensively. "The magic asked for nothing in return."

"The magic most certainly asked for something. It asked for experience. Sabrina broke her arm doing something I told her not to do. The healing is her experience of learning about the consequences for the choices she makes. Sure, it's easier to wave a wand or rub some magic medicine over our injuries. It's always easier. But what do we learn? How will Sabrina know her limitations?"

"Mom, you talk as if Sabrina and Daphne were normal little girls," Jake replied. "They're Grimms, and their lives are going to be difficult. Let the rest of the children learn about limitations. They don't have a Jabberwocky chasing their family. They need to be trained like Hank and I were, like Dad wanted."

"Your father was wrong," Granny Relda said. "The girls will explore the mirror's rooms when I say they are ready!"

"That's ridiculous!" her son complained.

"Is it, Jake? Is it still so hard to see after everything that has happened? Your father is dead because . . ." Granny Relda stopped midsentence, and there was a long silence between the two.

"You don't have to tell me why Dad is dead," Uncle Jake said. "I'm the one who killed him."

"Jake, I didn't mean . . ."

But Uncle Jake didn't let her finish. He turned, walked back down the hallway, and disappeared through the portal.

6

SABRINA AND DAPHNE FOLLOWED THEIR GRAND-mother into their bedroom. She said nothing, only pointed at the bed. The gesture spoke volumes.

"I think Uncle Jake is right," Sabrina said, though she knew she was pushing her luck with the old woman. "When are you going to teach us how to use the magic in the Hall of Wonders?"

The old woman cringed slightly, as if the question physically hurt her.

"We will discuss this later," she said.

"We're running out of time," Sabrina said. "Uncle Jake and I discovered Red Riding Hood's plan. She's trying to rebuild her lost family. She's got Mom and Dad and some poor family's baby. Next she's coming after you."

"That's not going to happen," Granny said, as she pulled the covers over the girls. "Nothing bad is going to happen to me."

"Can you guarantee that?" Sabrina pressed. "Because if you

can't, the two of us would be left alone in this town, and you saw how angry everyone got at the school. How would we protect ourselves?"

"Sabrina, stop!" Daphne whispered.

Sabrina's angry words rang in her own ears. It had been a heartless thing to say to her grandmother. She wished she could take it back.

The old woman looked stunned for a moment and then turned and exited the room without even a good-night.

"You know what? I have a question, Sabrina," Daphne said. "When are you going to stop acting like such a snot?"

"Daphne, you didn't see Red Riding Hood or the Jabberwocky," Sabrina grumbled. "I did, and Granny needs to take this seriously."

"You just accused her of not caring about us," Daphne said, then turned her back on her sister. She pulled the pillow from underneath her and put it over her head to block out Sabrina entirely.

The next morning Sabrina woke early in hopes of having some time alone with Uncle Jake. Maybe they could go through the journals and look for more information about Red Riding Hood and the Jabberwocky. Unfortunately, he was gone when she got downstairs. Instead, she found Granny Relda parked in her chair at the dining room table, sipping tea and writing in her journal.

When she saw Sabrina, she nodded stiffly, then returned to her writing. "I called the pharmacist to find out if there is anything we can do about the marker on your face," she said. "Unfortunately, it looks as if you're just going to have to be patient. She assured me the ink will fade in a couple of days."

Sabrina scowled. *A couple of days!*

"What do you want for breakfast?" the old woman asked, but before Sabrina could answer, Uncle Jake burst into the house and set a bright pink doughnut box on the table. He walked around the table and planted a big kiss on his mother's cheek.

"Hello, beautiful. I waited outside the Baker's shop for an hour. They're still warm."

"Doughnuts are not going to win me over," she said with a frown, but Sabrina could see that Uncle Jake's charm was working on her. Soon a grin began to form on her face. "Jake, the children need something healthy in the morning."

"I completely agree, but they can't live another day in this town without trying one of these," he said, turning to Sabrina. "The Baker makes them in the middle of the night, and if you're there when he opens the shop at five a.m., you can get them while they're fresh and hot. You should have seen the line! It was around the block! Even the Butcher and the Candlestick Maker were there, and those three can't stand one another."

"Being lost at sea in an old tub can strain a friendship," Granny explained. She reached in and took out a glazed doughnut. When she took a bite, a huge smile came to her face. "Oh, I've missed these."

"I know," Uncle Jake said with a laugh. "I've already had seven. I'm as hyper as a three-year-old, so I hiked up to the top of Mount Taurus. Sabrina, you have to go up there with me sometime. From the top, you can see the whole town. I had forgotten how beautiful Ferryport Landing is in winter."

Yeah, all four blocks of it, Sabrina thought. Still, it was an opportunity to visit the asylum again. Who knew what they might find?

Daphne and Elvis entered the dining room. "I smell doughnuts!" Daphne said. Elvis's tongue was hanging out and dripping drool on the floor.

"Help yourself," Uncle Jake said, opening the lid of the box. Daphne reached inside and took two doughnuts.

"Two?" Uncle Jake said with a grin.

"One's for Elvis," the little girl explained, tossing it into the air. The Great Dane leaped up and snatched it in midflight. Sabrina wondered if he even tasted it before he swallowed it whole.

Daphne bit into hers, then sank into her chair in a dreamlike state. "Oh . . . my . . . gosh," she mumbled with her mouth full.

"Sabrina?" Uncle Jake said, offering her the box. She reached in and took one. It was warm and sticky, all sugar and butter and love. Her first taste was like biting into pure happiness.

"Good, huh? Stick with me, girls. I know all of Ferryport Landing's best-kept secrets," he said with a wink. "Mom, I got to thinking. You said yesterday that you and the girls have been pretty busy since they arrived. That's a real shame. This town has a few interesting spots, and I bet they'd love to see some of the places where their dad and I used to hang out."

"You mean the places you two used to get into trouble?" she said knowingly.

"Exactly!" He leaned over and kissed the old woman on the cheek again. "It'll be fun."

Granny nodded reluctantly. "But not the asylum."

Jack shrugged. "Sure."

"Promise me, Jacob," the old woman insisted.

"Whatever you want, Mom," Uncle Jake said.

"Perhaps Mirror would like one of these doughnuts?" Granny asked.

"Mirror? I'm not wasting them on him," Jake argued.

"Jacob, Mirror is part of the family. Go give him one."

Jake scooped up the pink box and stomped out of the room.

Just then there was a knock at the door.

"Who could that be this early in the morning?" Granny wondered aloud.

When Sabrina opened the door, she was so surprised she nearly fell over. Mayor Charming was on the porch. Snow White stepped out from behind him, followed by his personal assistant, Mr. Seven, who was wearing the biggest grin she had ever seen.

"Sabrina, I know it's early, but I wanted to make sure you and your family were OK after what happened yesterday," Ms. White said.

"Oh, no harm done," said Granny, who had followed Sabrins to the door. She flashed the mayor a disappointed look.

"Oh, good. Billy has something he'd like to say. But first, he has to get ready. Mr. Seven, if you would be so kind."

The little man reached into his jacket pocket and took out a small wad of paper. He unfolded it quickly and handed it to the mayor. Sabrina recognized it at once. It was a paper hat with the words I AM AN IDIOT written on it in big black letters. The Mayor often forced Mr. Seven to wear it. Charming stared down at it with a scowl.

"Do I have to?" he groaned.

"Billy Charming!" Ms. White scolded. "You promised!"

The mayor set the hat squarely on his head. Sabrina couldn't help but laugh—not so much at Charming's humiliation, but at the expression of triumphant satisfaction on the face of his diminutive sidekick, Mr. Seven. The dwarf looked as if he had just won the lottery.

"I'm sorry," Charming whispered.

"I don't think they heard you," Snow said.

"Well, then they all need hearing aids!" Charming snapped.

"Billy! You said you would do the right thing, and if you don't, I will never speak to you again," Ms. White threatened. "And you know I mean it. We went a few hundred years without saying a word to each other!"

Charming sighed, and his broad shoulders and chest seemed to deflate right before Sabrina's eyes. "I'm sorry I turned on your family at the dedication ceremony yesterday."

Sabrina was stunned. Charming never apologized for anything as far as she knew, and she had two hundred years' worth of family journals to prove it. She began to realize just how much power Snow White held over the mayor.

"But you have to understand, this family is like a cancer that is threatening to eat me alive," Charming continued.

Ms. White gasped.

"Don't sugarcoat it, Mayor. Tell us how you really feel," Sabrina grumbled.

"The election is this weekend. I didn't expect to have an opponent this year. If the queen wasn't running, the only thing your presence would have given me was indigestion. But now that I might lose my job, the last thing I need is for the voters to start thinking I'm aligned with the Grimms. There's no time for damage control like that. I hardly have time to buy the votes I need and hire people to stuff ballot boxes . . ."

Ms. White's eyes flared with anger. The look was not lost on the mayor.

"I mean, get my message of hope out to the community," he finished.

"And the last thing you need is to look like you're buddy-buddy with a bunch of lowlifes like us," Sabrina replied sarcastically.

"See, Snow? The child understands!" Charming cried happily. "This hasn't been a good year for the town. The giant caused millions in property damage, and replacing the school cost millions more. Ferryport Landing is flat broke. Everafters and humans are starting to think a change would be good, and, trust me, the last thing you want is Mayor Heart running this town."

"I absolutely agree," Granny said. "If being anti-Grimm keeps you in office, then do what you have to do."

"Relda, I can't believe you," Snow White said with disappointment. "Do you know how hard it was to get him to apologize, and here you are encouraging his bad behavior!"

Uncle Jake came down the steps. "Ms. White, is that you?" he said, grinning from ear to ear.

Snow White looked at him with a curious expression. "I'm sorry. Have we met?"

"It's me, Jake Grimm. I was in your second-grade class. My brother, Henry, was a year ahead of me."

"*Your brother, Henry?*" Charming roared. "Relda, you never

told me you had another son. Every time I turn around there's another Grimm. You're like cockroaches. This town is infested!"

"William Charming!" Snow White roared angrily.

"You folks have a lovely day," Granny said, and closed the door in their faces.

"What did you do?" Uncle Jake asked her.

"I'm sure I don't know what you mean," Granny said to her son, as she turned and went back to the dining room. "I better start breakfast. Who wants waffles?"

Jake chased after her.

"Mom, Hamstead doesn't remember me, and he caught Hank and me skipping school a thousand times. Snow White doesn't remember me, even though I wrote her a love letter every day until I turned eighteen. Charming doesn't remember me, even though he put my face on wanted posters all over town."

"People forget things, Jake," Granny said. "It has been twelve years."

"Mom, I'm not bragging when I say this, but let's be honest: I'm pretty hard to forget!"

"What's going on?" Daphne asked.

Granny Relda looked like a cornered animal. Everyone was staring at her. Even Elvis cocked a curious eyebrow. She shuffled her feet and stammered a bit. "They don't remember you because I made them forget."

"You what?" Uncle Jake cried.

"When everyone found out what you did, there was chaos in the streets," Granny Relda said. "There was a mob outside my door for two weeks. People were getting hurt. I had to do something, so I had the whole town sprinkled with forgetful dust."

Sabrina couldn't believe what she was hearing.

"So everyone has forgotten me?" Uncle Jake asked.

"Not everyone," Granny said. "Mirror and Mr. Canis remember you."

"Mom, Mr. Canis is dead," Uncle Jake reminded her.

Granny flinched but regained her composure. "And Baba Yaga, of course," she continued. "Her house has spells to protect it from magic."

"Baba Yaga? Well, that's just great! A mentally deranged cannibal who collects human bones still remembers me. How did I get so lucky?"

Uncle Jake stomped out of the room, snatched his overcoat from the hall closet, and opened the front door.

"Where are you going?" Granny Relda asked.

"To warm up the car," he called. "Get your coats, girls, and try not to forget all about me before you get outside." He slammed the door behind him.

The girls stared at their grandmother, but she wouldn't meet their eyes.

"Is that the price for using magic you were talking about?" Sabrina asked.

Granny shuffled her feet.

"Granny, what did Uncle Jake do? Did he really kill his father?"

"Puck snuck in late last night. Sabrina, run up and invite him along. I'm sure he's feeling a bit left out."

Sabrina wanted to know more about what her Uncle Jake had done, but Granny Relda had an increasingly familiar expression on her face. The old woman didn't want to talk.

The last person in the world Sabrina wanted to invite anywhere was Puck. She reluctantly climbed the steps and knocked on his door several times, but there was no answer. She pushed it open and inspected the ground for catapults, bear traps, secret levers, and stink bombs. The coast seemed clear, so she stepped inside.

She called out for the prankster, but there was no response. After a couple more shouts she was ready to give up, but then she heard a *pop!* A stream of fire and smoke rose high in the sky and exploded into a thousand multicolored lights, followed by an ear-shaking *boom!* Puck was shooting off fireworks in his room. Moments later, another trail of smoke whistled into the sky. Their source seemed to be a hill beyond the lagoon.

The path was littered with broken toys and melted army men. Shattered marbles, stretched-out Slinkys, and the heads of some

Hungry Hungry Hippos were scattered everywhere. The mess ended in a clearing where Sabrina found Puck sitting on a jewel-encrusted toilet wearing his military medals. His chimpanzee army crowded around him, reaching for a box of matches he held in his hands, while the boy lectured them on the art of war.

"Johnson, step up here," he said. One of the chimps pushed through the crowd and approached the boy. "Johnson, the enemy is everywhere. Even your own men could be sympathetic to the enemy's cause. Would you be able take out your best friend if you were forced to?"

The chimp smiled widely, nodded, and clapped his hands.

"Johnson, you're a good soldier," Puck said. He lit a match and handed it to the furry creature. The lucky chimp raced over to a collection of fireworks of all shapes and sizes. Johnson lit the biggest red-and-white-striped rocket of the bunch and screamed with glee as it whistled into the air and exploded in the sky. When the lights and noise faded, the chimps hopped up and down in front of Puck and begged to be the recipient of the next match.

"Sullivan, front and center!" Puck commanded. "Tell me the first rule of war."

The chimp screamed and stomped its feet.

"That's right, Sullivan. Kill or be killed," Puck replied, handing him a match. Soon another rocket was flying overhead.

"What do you want?" Puck asked when he spotted Sabrina.

"We're going out with Uncle Jake. Granny says you have to go. We're waiting in the car. Unless you aren't done pouting."

"I'm not pouting," Puck said. "I'm busy turning these maggots into fighting machines."

The chimpanzees turned to him, baring their teeth and screaming impatiently for another match. Puck's head suddenly morphed into that of another chimp, and he hissed and spit at them. The chimps quieted, then went right back to begging for matches.

"Well, something's wrong. There are doughnuts in the dining room. Normally you'd have already wolfed them down and finished by licking the box."

"Who cares about doughnuts? I don't even like doughnuts," Puck said.

"You like everything. I've seen you eat Elvis's kibble right out of his bowl."

There was a long pause.

"Are they glazed?" he asked.

"Yes. Uncle Jake bought them," Sabrina said.

"I don't want anything from him."

"So this is about my uncle?"

"He's hogging the old lady. Just 'cause he's her real son," Puck replied.

"She hasn't seen him in twelve years, Puck," Sabrina pointed out.

"I don't care."

"Good."

"Good!"

There was a long silence.

"If you must know, I've been insulted," Puck explained.

"By who?"

"By all of you!" Puck cried. "I have an impeccable reputation as a scoundrel. I have been banned by thousands of hamlets, hundreds of cities, dozens of countries, and three different dimensions. There are bounties on my head in forty realms and on a few planets you've never heard of. I'm Puck, the Trickster King. I'm the mean and nasty emperor of pranksters. I'm the boy hero to nations of snickering layabouts. My kingdom is the wrong side of the tracks!"

"So?"

Puck snarled. "So? So? So, I threw it all away to protect this family, and not one of you cares. I'm ruined, and you have all turned your back on me for Uncle Jake. He'll save the family, blah, blah, blah!"

"Oh, stop being such a baby. Of course we care about you," Sabrina said.

"You care about me?"

"Yes, but don't let it go to your head, gasbag."

Puck sprang into the air, his wings flapping to keep him aloft.

"You're in love with me! I knew it!"

"Gross!"

"You want me to be your boyfriend, don't you?" Puck said.

Before she knew how to react, Puck flew to her side and kissed her . . . on the lips. The two separated and stared at each other for what felt like an eternity, and then Puck grinned and broke the silence. "I believe the words you are searching for are thank you."

And then Sabrina punched him in the belly.

Puck hunched over, gasping for breath.

"You try that again, you little freak, and you're going to need a dentist!" Sabrina shouted. She turned and stomped back down the path. She found the door to Puck's room, opened it, and slammed it behind her.

Leaning against the wall, Sabrina felt a million different things at once. Hot embarrassment was on her face, combined with frustration and bewilderment. Since she'd started noticing boys, she had dreamed about her first kiss. She'd imagined it would happen on a beach, or in a flower garden with a nice boy who really liked her. She'd never once, not even in her worst nightmares, thought that boy would be Puck, a dirty, smelly Everafter, surrounded by a bunch of screaming chimpanzee pyromaniacs.

It wasn't supposed to be Puck. He was annoying and mean. He dumped her in vats of disgusting glop. He put creepy crawlies in her bed. But the worst part of the kiss was that it was . . . nice.

She raced to the bathroom to see if her face looked different.

She looked flushed and embarrassed. Everyone would know she and Puck had kissed. It was practically written all over her face, as clear as the mustache and goatee the rotten jerk had drawn while she slept. She splashed herself with cool water and focused on catching her breath, and when she was ready, she gingerly walked back downstairs.

Daphne was tapping her foot at the bottom.

"Where's Puck?" the little girl asked.

"He's coming," Sabrina said as she pushed past her sister to get her coat from the closet.

"Did you two kiss and make up?"

Sabrina was sure her face was as red as a tomato. "C'mon, Uncle Jake is waiting," she said, and hurried outside, leaving Daphne behind.

Uncle Jake was leaning against the rusty old family car. It hadn't moved an inch since Mr. Canis's death.

Puck came out of the house to join them. He grinned at Sabrina, but she locked her eyes on her feet.

Uncle Jake extended his hand. "Glad to have you along, Puck," he said sincerely.

The boy sneered at the man and crawled into the backseat of the car. The girls followed, and the ancient car's shock absorbers groaned with complaint. Seeing Uncle Jake behind the wheel was strange to Sabrina, but when he inserted the key something even stranger happened—the car didn't backfire. Every time Canis drove, the big pile of junk let loose a series of ear-shattering explosions that could be heard in the next county. This time it rumbled softly like a brand-new car. Sabrina saw her own surprise mirrored in her sister's face.

"How did you do that?" Daphne asked.

"I have a way with women," Uncle Jake said, caressing the dusty dashboard. "Genevieve and I understand one another."

"Genevieve?" Sabrina cried.

"That's her name. I left her here when I left town. Your father and I got into a lot of trouble in this car."

He put "Genevieve" in reverse and backed it out into the street. Soon they were tooling along the back roads of Ferryport Landing. What Sabrina had always thought of as the world's dullest town took on a whole new light when her uncle talked about it. Every mailbox, abandoned house, graffiti-covered bridge, and broken window had a story. The more the girls heard, the more it became clear that Uncle Jake and their straitlaced father were once first-class juvenile delinquents. Sabrina was fascinated, especially with the stories that included magical elements: The boys once cast a gigantic spell on the Three Blind Mice and watched them stagger around town, they poured a rusting potion onto the Tin Woodsman, and they even found a way to give the Old Woman Who Lived in a Shoe athlete's foot. Jake and Sabrina's father were troublemakers on par with Puck himself. Which made the boy's dislike for her uncle all the more puzzling. After all, the two had so much in common. Puck was clearly unimpressed with Uncle Jake's stories of mischief. He sat in the backseat with his arms crossed, acting as if he weren't paying attention. Sabrina did her best to act as if she didn't notice. Every time the boy looked at her she felt like her face was on fire.

After a couple hours of sightseeing, Uncle Jake made a turn that led up to an empty field. He parked the car when they were far enough away from the road that no one could see them.

"What are we doing here?" Daphne asked as everyone got out of the car.

"It's time for your first lesson," Uncle Jake replied, leading the children to the center of the open field. "Mom doesn't want you messing with the stuff in the Hall of Wonders, but I have a few goodies of my own. I'm going to teach you to use some of them. Puck, would you like to learn something, too?"

Puck sneered. "I know all I'm gonna."

Uncle Jake dug in his pockets and produced Merlin's wand. He handed it to Daphne, but she refused to take it.

"No, thank you," she said.

Her uncle was surprised. "Daphne, you could use this to save your mom and dad and keep you and your sister safe. Your grandmother never has to know."

Daphne shook her head.

"Looks like you're going to be the hero," Uncle Jake said to Sabrina as he handed the wand to her. As soon as she touched it, she felt the familiar charge run through her body. It was exhilarating. "OK, the name of the game with a magic wand is control. It's a challenge to aim and concentrate all at once. The thing about monsters is they don't wait until you're ready, so you need practice."

Sabrina nodded, doing her best to avoid Daphne's disapproving glare.

"So you've seen how it works for garland and tinsel," Uncle Jake said. "Let's try something with a little more punch. Let's pretend those trees over there are the Jabberwocky. We need something really big to knock one down. It could be anything, but let's try lightning. To get some lightning, think about the worst thunderstorm you've ever seen, a really scary one with fierce wind and rain."

Sabrina closed her eyes and immediately remembered the night after her parents disappeared. There had been a terrible thunderstorm right outside of their apartment windows. The girls slept in their mom and dad's bed, hoping they'd come home soon, but they never did. Every lightning strike shook the building.

"Nice job, kiddo. Take a look," Uncle Jake said.

Sabrina opened her eyes and found an identical thunderstorm gathering in the sky above her. Static energy crackled in the air and caused the hair on her arms to rise. She felt supercharged, like she was filled with enough power to do anything she could imagine, like there was nothing that could hurt her. All of her fears and worries about Red Riding Hood and the Jabberwocky faded away, and for the first time in a year and a half she felt calm and confident. It was a sensation so incredible she wondered if there was a way to feel it all the time.

"Now aim and say, 'Gimme some lightning.'"

Sabrina did as she was told. "Gimme some lightning!" she shouted.

A bolt of lightning plummeted to the earth and crashed into the bank of trees. They disappeared for a moment in a flash of brilliant white light, which was followed by an earth-shaking *boom!* When it was over, one of the trees was cracked in half and on fire.

"Nice shot," Uncle Jake said. "I think you're a natural."

"Could lightning kill the Jabberwocky?" Sabrina asked. She imagined unleashing the wand's power on the monster and smiled.

"Lightning won't kill it," Uncle Jake said. "But it would knock the ugly sucker off its feet, hopefully long enough to get your parents back."

Just then, one of Puck's pixie minions zipped across the field. It stopped at Puck's ear and buzzed excitedly. Puck's eyes lit up, and his wings popped out of his back. He drew his sword and peered toward the woods.

"There's someone in the forest watching us," he said, as he lifted off the ground and flew toward the tree line.

The Grimms plunged into its thick brush after Puck, and Sabrina quickly caught a glimpse of someone running far ahead—a man. His speed was superhuman, and she watched him leap effortlessly over a downed tree. Before they could get a good look at him, he was gone.

"I'm going to follow him!" Puck shouted, zipping into the woods.

"Be careful!" Sabrina called out.

"What would be the fun in that?" Puck said as he disappeared into the forest.

"I hate to admit it, but he's a lot like your dad and me," Uncle Jake said. "I can see why you and Mom love him so much."

"Love him? I don't love him. He's a pain in the butt!" Sabrina shouted, a bit louder than she intended. It made her even more embarrassed.

"Did anyone see that guy's face?" Daphne asked.

Uncle Jake shook his head. "Maybe he's one of those Scarlet Hand weirdos."

"Maybe," Sabrina said. The thought made her worry for Puck, which made her feel ridiculous. Since when did she worry about stinky Puck? She wanted to dig a hole and bury herself.

❧

The group waited an hour and a half before they gave up on Puck. The boy could always fly home, so they got into the old car without him and cruised back down to the town. As they passed a diner, Uncle Jake slammed on the brakes and abruptly pulled into the parking lot.

"This place is the best!" he cried.

Sabrina had spotted the Blue-Plate Special several times since her move to Ferryport Landing. It was right next door to the Ferryport Landing post office. A neon sign of a grinning waitress holding a bright-blue tray of burgers and shakes lit up the street. It was the kind of place her parents would have taken Sabrina and Daphne to after a movie or a visit to the Central Park Zoo. Sabrina remembered the old-fashioned egg creams her father loved so much, and she was thrilled to see them on the menu. Granny had told her the diner employed a lot of Everafters, but she didn't mind. She just hoped they knew how to make disco fries.

The inside of the restaurant was decorated for the holiday season, with little Christmas trees painted on the windows and a menorah on the counter. There were booths along a bank of windows, each with a personal jukebox, and customers drinking coffee and reading the newspaper. A dessert case in the corner spun slowly, tempting Sabrina with cheesecake dripping with strawberry sauce, and chocolate parfaits. Overworked waitresses rushed from table to table, shouting their odd diner-speak to the short-order cooks in the kitchen. The place smelled like hamburgers and mashed potatoes, and Sabrina knew everything would taste a little like chicken. She was in heaven.

At a table at the far end of the restaurant sat Mr. Swineheart and Mr. Boarman. They set down their coffee cups and waved to the group. The girls waved back, then slid into a booth near the door with Uncle Jake. They each snatched a menu from behind the ketchup caddy and scanned it eagerly.

"I swear, I'm going to eat everything on this menu," Daphne said. "Who wants onion rings?"

Uncle Jake didn't respond. He gazed around the room, looking depressed.

"Uncle Jake?" Sabrina said.

"We used to come here when I was a kid. Hank and I would collect old soda bottles and take them to Tweedledee and Tweedledum's convenience store for the deposits. Then we'd head over here and drink chocolate malts all day. This was our booth. That waitress at the door—her name is Farrah, and she owns this place. We used to drive her nuts, but she doesn't even recognize me. That man at the counter—he's the Scarecrow. He runs the town library. I owe him probably forty dollars in late fees. Over in that booth by the window is the Cheshire Cat—we once watched a pit bull chase him up a tree. The fire department had to come and get him down. He called us 'a couple of no-good hooligans' for laughing."

Sabrina turned around. The man Uncle Jake was referring to was studying his menu. He had the biggest eyes and grin Sabrina had ever seen.

"But I've been erased." Uncle Jake sighed.

"What did you do?" Daphne asked.

He shifted uncomfortably in his chair. "Something very, very stupid."

"How y'all doin'?" a waitress said as she bopped over to the table with an order pad and pencil in hand. She had a big out-of-date hairdo, bright pink lipstick, and a name tag that read FARRAH. "What can I getcha?" she asked, between chomps on her bubble gum.

"I'll have a grilled cheese with bacon and tomato," Uncle Jake said. "You still make those fantastic chocolate malts?"

"You bet we do," Farrah said. "Sounds like you've been here before."

"A couple times." Uncle Jake sighed.

"And what about you, honey?" Farrah asked, turning to Sabrina. Waitresses in Manhattan were always calling her "honey." It made her a little homesick.

Sabrina read her order straight from the menu. "Cheeseburger, medium, disco fries, an egg cream, and . . ."

"What'cha lookin' for, darlin'?" Farrah asked.

"Oh, I wish you had blueberry cobbler. There was a diner near our apartment in Manhattan that specialized in it."

"Well, we do." Farrah pointed to the dessert list. There was BLUEBERRY COBBLER in black and white. Sabrina could have sworn it hadn't been there a moment ago. "Looks like you've got the four major food groups covered. How about you, short stuff?"

"I want chicken wings, macaroni and cheese, and jalapeño poppers," Daphne said.

Farrah jotted it down.

"Then, for my main course, I would like the overstuffed Reuben sandwich with extra Thousand Island dressing, a side of tater tots, a black-and-white milkshake, and a cherry vanilla Dr Pepper."

"Sweetie, you can't eat all that." Farrah laughed.

"Oh, she'll eat it," Sabrina said. "We call her The Stomach."

"Save me a slice of cheesecake, too," Daphne added after she stuck out her tongue at her sister.

Farrah laughed, shoved her pencil behind her ear, and headed to the back with the order.

The door jingled, and a crowd of people entered the diner. Leading them was the Queen of Hearts and Sheriff Nottingham, though they were dressed in regular clothing. The queen called out a hello to everyone, while members of her entourage handed out VOTE FOR HEART buttons. The queen and the sheriff went from table to table, shaking hands with people and asking for votes.

Sabrina frowned, knowing it was just a matter of time before the duo got to their table.

"Maybe we should leave," she said.

"Leave?" Daphne gasped. "Do you know how long it has been since I had chicken wings?"

"No, this will be fun," Uncle Jake said, just as Mrs. Heart and Nottingham reached their table. Without even looking, the queen took Uncle Jake's hand and shook it vigorously while her handlers pinned campaign buttons on the girls without bothering to ask if it was OK.

"Hello, everyone, my name is Heart and I'm running for mayor of Ferryport Landing," the woman said.

"Hello, Your Majesty," Uncle Jake said with a mischievous grin.

The queen's eyes quickly darted to Uncle Jake's face and immediately flared with rage.

"You!" she cried, yanking her hand away as if she had just put it inside a hornet's nest.

"Us," Daphne said.

"How is the campaign going?" Uncle Jake asked.

"It's going just fine, thank you," Mrs. Heart seethed. "Your assault on the community yesterday only helped get my point across. There's not enough room in this town for Everafters and Grimms."

"What an inspiring message of hope," Uncle Jake replied.

Sheriff Nottingham grabbed Jake by the collar and pulled him close to his angry face. "Laugh now, boy, but when we're running this town, I will personally squash your filthy vermin family under my boot heels," he barked.

"Take your hands off my uncle," Sabrina said.

Nottingham snarled. "Shut your gob, child, or I'll smack it off your face."

"What does *gob* mean?" Daphne asked.

Sabrina shrugged, reached into her pocket, took out the wand, and aimed it at the sheriff.

"Do you know what this is?" she asked.

Nottingham stared at the wand. "I don't have the foggiest," he growled.

"It's Merlin's wand," Sabrina said as she watched fear flash in Nottingham's eyes. Sabrina smiled as she felt an overwhelming urge to zap the man with a shot of lightning. "My uncle just taught me how to use it."

Nottingham let Jake go and stepped back from the table, but Sabrina kept pointing the wand at him. It felt good to let the bad guys know she was powerful.

Just then, everyone's attention was stolen by an enormous thump. It knocked the ketchup bottle off the table and nearly caused the Scarecrow to fall off his stool. It was followed by another, the source of which seemed to come from outside. Everyone turned to look out at the parking lot where they saw a car flip over and crash into another. A moment later another car got the same destructive treatment.

Farrah approached with a tray of food and set the edge of it on the table. "Chow time!" she sang cheerily, but her voice trailed off when she saw the destruction through the window. "Oh my."

"What is that, Nottingham?" the queen demanded.

The would-be sheriff pointed out the window. "I think it's her."

Little Red Riding Hood skipped through the parking lot like a happy schoolgirl, holding a leash, on the end of which walked her monstrous, reptilian playmate. The two demented creatures were coming straight for the diner.

"Everyone remain calm," Nottingham said confidently, just as the rest of the diners leaped from their seats and hid under the tables. An older gentleman jumped from his chair at the counter and knocked into Farrah, who spilled the family's meals all over the floor.

Nottingham opened his coat and pulled a sword from a scabbard strapped around his waist. He pointed it at the Jabberwocky, but it made no impression on the beast. The hulking brute grabbed the front wall of the diner and tore it away as if it were paper. It poked its gruesome head into the hole, mere inches away from Sabrina and Daphne, and flicked its tongue around as if it were tasting the fear in the air.

"JABBERWOCKY!" the monster cried.

7

WHERE'S MY GRANDMOTHER?" RED RIDING Hood screamed. Her face was a contorted mess, like a sculpture made from Silly Putty whose features were twisted and stretched into horrible exaggerations. "I want to play!"

Jake and the girls tumbled out of the booth, and the wand slipped from Sabrina's grasp. It bounced on the floor, then rolled to the other side of the room. She was ready to go after it when her uncle pulled her back.

"Stay down," he whispered.

Others were not so smart. Nottingham raised his sword and waved it in the air threateningly. "Child," he said to Red Riding Hood, "take this overgrown tadpole and go, or I swear I'll—"

But his threat was never finished. The Jabberwocky whipped its tail at him. Nottingham sailed across the room and into the dessert case. He let out a terrible groan and collapsed to the floor.

"Grandmother, are you in there?" the little girl called out, as she and the Jabberwocky stepped through the hole and into the diner. She searched every face with growing disappointment while patrons cowered under tables.

"Who are you looking for, young lady?" Mrs. Heart called out with a trembling voice.

"My grandmother," Red Riding Hood said. Her face suddenly went from rage to a sweet hopeful smile.

"Oh, you poor thing," the queen said as she forced a smile to her face. "You're so confused. Your grandmother is dead. Don't you remember? She was eaten by the Big Bad Wolf."

Red Riding Hood sputtered and rocked back and forth on her heels. "That's not true. That's not true," she said to herself, over and over again. "She's just hiding. We're playing a game. I have to find her so my family can be together again."

The Jabberwocky leaned down to Red and licked her face with its long, disgusting tongue, causing her to giggle. "Oh, kitty, are you bored? Do you want to play? I bet this lady would like to play with you."

The Jabberwocky gnashed its teeth enthusiastically and turned to Mrs. Heart. It snatched her off the ground in one of its huge claws, and she screamed and begged for mercy.

"Do something!" Sabrina whispered to her uncle. She didn't like the Queen of Hearts, not even a little, but she didn't want her to die, either.

Uncle Jake rolled his eyes and sighed. "Fine," he grumbled. He sprang to his feet and pointed a threatening finger at the brute. "Hey, ugly—put her down, or I won't tell you where the grandmother and the puppy are hiding."

"You know my grandmother?" Red Riding Hood asked.

"Yes, yes!" the queen cried as she struggled to free herself. "He's the one you want! Not me! There's no need to kill me!"

The Jabberwocky gnashed its fangs and dropped the Queen of Hearts. It stomped across the room toward the Grimms, tossing tables and chairs out of its way.

"Uncle Jake? It's coming," Sabrina cried, panicked.

"I'm working on it, kid," Uncle Jake said. He frantically searched his many pockets for something that he could use against the monster. Pennies, buttons, half a candy bar, and dozens of trinkets and necklaces were tossed aside. "I have just the thing in here. Where on earth did I put it?" But he never found whatever he was searching for. The monster backhanded him so hard he crashed through the men's room door.

The Jabberwocky beat on its chest and flapped its leathery wings. It shrieked and spat as chaos ensued. The monster stomped its colossal foot on the floor, causing a shockwave to roll through the diner. Chairs flew through the ceiling and walls, exploding into the dessert case right above the still unconscious Nottingham. Several cups of butterscotch pudding tipped over and dribbled down onto his head.

"Stay put," Sabrina told her sister, then scrambled across the room after her wand. Just as she snatched it up, the Jabberwocky leaped forward and set a heavy paw on her chest, pinning her arms at her side. She couldn't move an inch. The monster bent down so that its nose was touching Sabrina's, and it sprayed its hot, pungent breath into her face.

"Fine! I give up. You've beaten me, Grimm. Are you happy?"

"Puck?" she cried.

She heard flapping wings above her. The sound infuriated the Jabberwocky, which turned to face the boy, freeing Sabrina. She crawled back to her hiding sister, and together they got to their feet. Once there, she saw Puck's beautiful pink-streaked wings fluttering around the room. He pulled back on a slingshot loaded with a broken brick and let it fly. It smacked into one of the Jabberwocky's eyes, and the beast shrieked.

"You dragged me into this hero business against my will, and now every time I turn around, I'm saving the day. Well, I hope you're happy."

"Are you expecting me to apologize because you're doing a good deed?" Sabrina asked.

Red Riding Hood screamed. "I don't want to play this game!"

"Hey, let's play the quiet game!" Puck shouted at the little girl. "Your crazy talk is distracting me from my heroics."

Instantly, the Jabberwocky lunged at Puck and knocked the boy out of the sky. Puck fell hard to the ground, unable to defend himself as the monster reached down and grabbed hold of him with one hand. It lifted Puck up to its face and examined him closely.

"Don't worry, girls," Puck shouted sarcastically. "I'll save you!"

With one lightning-fast motion, the Jabberwocky reached over, grabbed hold of Puck's fairy wings, and ripped them off his back. The sound was excruciating, and Puck cried out in agony before he lost consciousness.

"Puck!" the girls shouted.

The Jabberwocky tossed him hard against a wall. He didn't get back up.

Sabrina felt as if the world were spinning in slow motion. A terrifying sense of helplessness came over her. It was the same despair she'd felt in so many of her recent nightmares, and she was tired of it. She squeezed Merlin's wand in her hand and suddenly felt like she had plugged into a light socket. Her blood was replaced with a current. She could have sworn at that moment that her eyes were on fire and she was a hundred feet tall. The amount of raw energy she had at her disposal was incredible. She aimed the wand at the monster, and storm clouds filled the air. Lightning crackled, and a bolt of white energy shot out of the sky and hit the Jabberwocky in the chest. There was an enormous explosion, and the monster fell onto its back. A smoldering black burn appeared where the lightning had struck the beast.

Sabrina was shocked when the Jabberwocky stirred and crawled to its feet. "You want some more? Fine!" she shouted. Another lightning blast caught the monster on the top of its head. It fell to the ground again. This time she took a step closer, only to have the beast's head curl toward her, its teeth gnashing and eager to bite her. Now she was shaking, not from fear but from anger at the monster's defiance. How dare this thing continue to live!

She shook the wand angrily and summoned another crash of lightning, and another, and another, until her ears rang from the deafening thunder that came with every bolt. "Stay down!" she shouted, unable to hear her own words, but the monster refused. It got up, again and again and again, and each time it took a step closer to her.

Finally, the smoking hulk backed her into a corner. Covered in cuts and burns, it shrieked into her face. She knew she had failed and braced for the monster's attack, but the Jabberwocky was suddenly lifted off its feet and slammed to the ground.

The impact sent the girls tumbling over each other.

"I didn't do that," Sabrina said, staring down at the wand.

"Then who did?" Daphne cried.

"Doggy!" Red Riding Hood shouted.

Sabrina turned to see what the evil girl was screaming about. There, standing over the monster, was a rail-thin man wearing a suit several sizes too big for him. He had watery eyes and feeble hands. He also had a shock of white unruly hair. Sabrina knew his face, but it wasn't possible. He was dead!

"Mr. . . . Canis?" Sabrina stammered.

There was something different about him. He had bright blue eyes—the same color as those of his alter ego, the Big Bad Wolf.

"Stay down, girls," he growled.

The Jabberwocky fought its way to its feet and tore into Mr. Canis, pounding its huge paws into the old man's chest. Despite the horrific blows, he seemed more than capable of handling the monster's abuse and dished out some of his own. One swing from his fist sent the Jabberwocky sailing through the hole in the diner's wall and into the parking lot. Cars went flying, and pavement crumbled under its skidding body.

"Look! The doggy and the kitty are playing!" Red Riding Hood shouted gleefully.

Sabrina pointed Merlin's wand at the deranged little girl.

"Where are my parents, you little psychopath?"

The little girl snarled like a wild animal. "They're *my* parents!" she raged.

"You tell me right now, or I'm going to fry you," Sabrina threatened. Clouds formed in the sky outside. She could hear the rumble of thunder. With a single thought, the little girl would be a stain on the floor.

"I almost have my whole family!" Red Riding Hood screamed in anger.

"You're asking for it!" Sabrina threatened, but suddenly the wand was knocked out of her hand. She turned to face her attacker and found Daphne standing next to her.

"Sabrina, no!"

"Tell my grandmother I'm coming. Tell her I have a basket of goodies for her!" Red Riding Hood shouted as the ring on her finger cast a crimson light on the room. A moment later, both she and the Jabberwocky disappeared into thin air.

"How could you, Daphne? She's got Mom and Dad!"

Daphne waved her off. "Puck needs our help."

The two girls rushed to the fallen fairy's side, but Mr. Canis was already lifting his wounded body into his arms. "I will get him help, girls. You and Jacob need to get home now," he said roughly, then dashed away at an amazing speed. Sabrina had never seen anyone, man or Everafter, run so fast.

Uncle Jake was still unconscious. Farrah stood over him with a glass of water.

"Don't worry, girls," she said as she tossed the water into his face. "We get a lot of drunks in here around two a.m. This works every time."

Uncle Jake bolted upright and looked around. "What did I miss?"

"Let's just put it this way," Farrah said. "It's going to be a little while on the blueberry cobbler."

After Glinda the Good Witch scattered forgetful dust on the bewildered human diner customers and Sheriff Hamstead checked to make sure everyone was OK, the family got a high-speed police escort back home.

"Granny!" Sabrina shouted as they ran into the house.

The old woman was upstairs, and she called down to them. The girls and the sheriff found her in her bedroom sitting next to Puck, who was buried under blankets. The boy looked pale and weak.

"Is he going to be all right?" Sabrina asked.

"I don't know," Granny said. "He's seriously injured."

"Mr. Canis is alive," Daphne said.

Granny nodded and tilted her head to the corner. There they saw Mr. Canis, resting in a chair and looking exhausted. The old man had never been the picture of health, but now he looked especially bad. His eyes were bloodshot, and his face seemed to be hanging onto his head for dear life.

Sabrina turned to her grandmother. "Did you know he was still alive?"

Granny Relda nodded. "Yes."

"You lied to us! How could you? I've been blaming myself for his death."

"I asked her to keep it a secret," Canis said. "I wanted to save you from myself."

"I don't understand," Daphne said.

"It's happening again, isn't it?" Hamstead asked.

Mr. Canis stood and turned, revealing a furry brown tail popping out of the back of his trousers.

"You're losing control of the Wolf," Sabrina said.

"Something I cannot allow," he said.

"Then what are you going to do about it?" Daphne asked.

The old man looked at the floor. The answer seemed to pain him.

"You're planning on killing yourself, aren't you?" Sabrina whispered.

"I would rather die than let the Wolf loose again. Every one of his victims lives inside my mind. I hear them beg for mercy that never came. I see the terror in their faces as they died. His crimes are still destroying lives, including your own. You've seen today the repercussions of his violence."

"Little Red Riding Hood," Sabrina said.

"I took the girl's family from her," Mr. Canis whispered. "I drove her insane."

Sheriff Hamstead turned to the girls. "When the Everafters came over on Jacob and Wilhelm's ship, Red spent the entire voyage raving to herself, drawing these horrible pictures, and screaming through the night. Even the ogres were terrified of her. It was obvious she was sick, so when we got settled in Ferryport Landing, our first order of business was finding a place to keep her. We built the asylum at the top of Mount Taurus and hired a few Everafter doctors and nurses to look after her, but she kept finding ways to escape, so something had to be done. Spaulding Grimm went to Baba Yaga and asked her to cast the same spell on the asylum that she'd used to trap everyone in the town."

"You locked her up?" Daphne asked.

"Daphne, you have to understand. There was so much to do—settling and building the town, making sure people didn't starve, keeping our secret. There wasn't any time left for one sick child."

"But it wasn't just one sick child," Granny said. "Anyone who became a serious problem was sent to the asylum."

"Or anything. We put the Jabberwocky there as well," Sheriff Hamstead added.

"Wait, if the spell on the asylum is the same kind as the one around the town, how did Red Riding Hood get loose?" Sabrina asked.

Granny Relda turned to Uncle Jake. He seemed to sink into his clothing.

"Tell them, Mom. They deserve to know," he said.

Granny's face looked pained, but she took a few deep breaths and stood up from the bed. She turned to one of the framed photos on the wall. It was of her and the girls' grandpa Basil when the two were much younger. Sabrina guessed they were in their mid-twenties. Even though the photo was in black and white, it couldn't hide the color in their faces. Their eyes and cheeks glowed. They were young and in love. Granny took the photo off the wall and looked at it lovingly.

"Oh, where to start? When I was twenty-six I met a man at a party in Berlin. A week later I married him. His name was Basil Grimm.

"I didn't know anything about the Grimm family, really, other than what I had learned about Jacob and Wilhelm in school. All I knew was that Basil was a handsome, adventurous, slightly arrogant American who swept me off my feet. He told me we were going on a honeymoon. It would be the last vacation we ever took, but we packed memories into it that would last a lifetime. We traveled the globe together on a two-year adventure.

"We went everywhere: Istanbul, Hawaii, Alaska, Tibet, the Amazon, South Africa, the Galápagos Islands—it was exhilarating. Every morning we woke up in a strange new land, hungry to explore. These were some of the happiest times of my life. A year into the trip I got pregnant with your father, but we continued to travel even after he was born."

Granny put the photo back and crossed the room to where another framed photo hung. This one was of the couple in a snowy landscape, riding a dogsled. She took it off the wall and admired it.

"Before the two years were quite up, Basil got a letter from his sister Matilda telling him to come home. Basil's brother, your great-uncle Edwin, had passed away, so we came to Ferryport Landing as quickly as we could, and I was introduced to the family business."

Granny put the photo back on the wall.

"Your uncle Jake was born a year later, shortly after Matilda passed away from pneumonia. Basil was proud of his boys and was determined that they would carry on the family responsibility. Even when they were babies, he would stand over their cribs and read them the family journals. When they were five and six, he set them loose in the Hall of Wonders, giving them free rein and their own sets of keys. When other boys their age were playing baseball, Henry and Jacob were playing with magic wands and flying carpets and dragons. By the time they were young men, they were as adept at magical weaponry and lore as any Everafter in the town."

Uncle Jake cleared his throat. "I'll take it from here, Mom." He turned to the girls. "When your father turned twenty, he fell in love with someone. This was before he met your mother. She was an Everafter, and it broke his heart to know she was trapped in this town. It broke my heart to see him so sad. I wanted to give him something special. So I turned off the barrier so she could escape."

Everyone gasped, especially Sheriff Hamstead. "How?" he squealed.

"I snuck into Baba Yaga's house and found her spell book. The spell I discovered was simple, and it would shut the barrier down, but only for a moment. It was all I needed. Hank's girlfriend waited on the outskirts of town, and when the spell took effect she stepped through to freedom. Neither of us could wait to see Hank's face when he saw her waving to him from the other side. Unfortunately, we had no idea what would happen.

"Dropping the barrier also dropped the spell on the asylum," Uncle Jake explained. "Everyone inside was free, including Red and the Jabberwocky. When I discovered what I'd done, I went after the monster. I chased it through the forest without even thinking about what I would do if I caught it. Predictably, it found me, and it cornered me on a cliff."

"And his father came to save him," Granny Relda said.

"He never came home again," Uncle Jake said, turning away from the group. "Hamstead and his deputies found him and took him to the hospital, but there was nothing they could do. He died a day later, and the monster disappeared into the woods along with Red Riding Hood."

"My men and I have been looking for them ever since," Hamstead said.

Granny's face was full of fresh heartbreak. Sabrina could see that reliving this old story felt just as tragic to the old woman as it had the day her husband died.

"Your father was distraught, so he left for New York City the day after the funeral," Granny Relda said. "He met your mother not long after, and she helped him heal his broken heart. When he moved back home, she came with him. They married, and Veronica was inducted into the family business just like I was, but each mystery they uncovered unnerved your father in ways he'd never experienced before. He worried something would happen to his new bride, and when she announced she was pregnant with you, Sabrina, he packed their things and they left town. He told me his children deserved to have a normal life, that you and Daphne would have nothing to do with magic, Everafters, or the Hall of Wonders. He didn't want you to lose him, the way he'd lost Basil."

"I left town after the funeral, too," Jake said. "I couldn't face what I had done or the people whose lives I had wrecked. I didn't know about Henry and Veronica. I didn't know you girls were in an orphanage. I didn't even know Canis was in an accident. I abandoned you all."

"Why don't I remember any of this happening?" Sheriff Hamstead asked suspiciously.

"I'm sorry, Ernest. I made you forget," Relda responded. "When news spread that there was a way to drop the barrier, things got very ugly. There were riots. People were getting hurt, and I had to find a way to stop it. I dusted the whole town."

"I suppose I can't be angry. I've scattered a lot of forgetful dust myself," the sheriff said. "Any other big secrets, Relda?"

The old woman grinned uncomfortably.

Sabrina looked down at Puck. He was fevered, pale, and unconscious. "What can we do for him?" she asked.

"I don't know," Granny replied. "He's not human. He needs a doctor who's familiar with fairies, but I don't believe we have one in this town."

"We can't let him die," Daphne said, as tears spilled onto her cheeks.

"I hope your 'no magic' rule isn't getting in the way of helping him," Sabrina said.

Granny pointed to a collection of empty tins, tubes, and bottles on the nightstand. "In an emergency, magic makes sense. Unfortunately, nothing we have is working."

"Then we'll try something else," Sabrina insisted.

"And we will fail, child," Mr. Canis said. "Puck is not like you. He's not even like most of the Everafters, creatures touched by magic. He's a creature made of magic."

"Then what? We just give up? We have to do something!"

"He needs to be with his own people. He needs to be in the fairy homeland," the old man said. "They will know how to help him."

"Let's go!" Daphne cried.

"We can't," Granny said.

"The barrier," Sabrina whispered as she lowered her eyes. Puck was lying there in front of her, probably dying, all because of some stupid two-hundred-year-old spell.

"Wait, you said you knew how to turn off the barrier," Hamstead said to Uncle Jake.

"Absolutely not," Granny Relda said before her son could answer. "Red Riding Hood and the Jabberwocky escaped from the asylum when the barrier fell the first time. We can't risk them escaping the town, too."

"I have an idea that could solve all our problems," Uncle Jake said.

Everyone turned to him and listened.

"The Vorpal blade," he continued.

"You mean that thing Mr. Van Winkle mentioned the other day?" Daphne asked.

"Lewis Carroll wrote about it in *Through the Looking Glass*. It's a magical sword and supposedly the only thing that can kill a Jabberwocky."

"He's right," Sabrina added. "I read about it in the family journals. It not only killed the other Jabberwockies, it also cut a hole in the barrier. The Black Knight used it to escape Ferryport Landing. We could use it to help Puck do the same thing!"

"We could also use it to kill the Jabberwocky," Uncle Jake said, "and rescue Hank and Veronica."

"Well, what are we waiting for?" Daphne cried.

Granny Relda lowered her eyes. "Spaulding Grimm had the Vorpal blade destroyed. He believed the sword was too dangerous to keep around. He broke it and hid the pieces around the town. Unfortunately, he never wrote down where he hid them. He took the secret of their whereabouts to his grave."

Sabrina's heart sank. Puck would certainly die now.

"Except for one," Granny finished. She opened a drawer in her nightstand and took out a swatch of green velvet. Inside was something long and heavy. She placed it in Uncle Jake's hands.

He unwrapped the object and revealed a piece of shiny steel attached to an ornate hilt.

"What are we going to do with a broken sword?" Daphne asked.

"I don't know," Granny replied. "But maybe we can find the other pieces. There's an inscription on the hilt I believe provides a clue."

Uncle Jake read it. "Find the daughter of the water."

"Who's the daughter of the water?" Sabrina asked.

Granny shrugged.

"Even if you find this daughter of the water and get the other pieces, is there someone in this town who can put the sword back together?" Hamstead interjected.

"The legend of the Vorpal blade says the sword was indestructible," Uncle Jake said. "Clearly, Spaulding found a way to break it. He needed someone with seriously powerful mojo to help—maybe that person can put it back together again. There's only one person in this town who can do something like that."

"The Blue Fairy," Canis said.

"From the Pinocchio story?" Daphne asked.

"The same. The Blue Fairy has magic like no other Everafter. She can grant any wish. She once turned a wooden doll into a real boy. Even Baba Yaga doesn't have the power of life. Putting the Vorpal blade back together should be easy for her."

"So, problem solved. We'll find the other pieces and take them to the Blue Fairy," Sabrina said.

"Except no one knows who the Blue Fairy is," Granny Relda said.

"You've got to be kidding me," Daphne said. "We don't know the identity of the most powerful Everafter in this town?"

"The spell she uses to disguise herself is flawless. I suppose I would want my privacy, too, if I could grant wishes and bring things to life. People would want to take advantage of a power like that."

"This is crazy," Daphne cried. "Even if we find the pieces, we can't put them together. We can't kill the Jabberwocky or get Puck to his people."

"This is not crazy, *liebling*. It's a mystery, and we're Grimms.

This is what we do," Granny said, wrapping her arms around the little girl's shoulders.

"I'll return to the forest and continue to track the girl and the monster," Mr. Canis said as he stood up slowly. "I feel stronger in the woods, anyway."

"I've got to get a handle on what happened at the diner," Hamstead said. "If too many humans drive by and see the destruction, I'll have to dust the whole town, too. Keep me in the loop about any progress you make. C'mon, old friend. I'll give you a ride."

The Sheriff and Canis left the room.

"We should get started on research, girls," Uncle Jake said. "I'm sure if we dig into the journals, we'll find some reference to this daughter of the water."

"I've had that piece of the sword for decades, and I've had a lot of time to research. I still can't imagine what Spaulding meant," Granny Relda said.

"Maybe it's a fish," Daphne said.

Uncle Jake and Granny shared a look, then smiled at Daphne like she was one of the seven wonders of the world.

"Daphne, you're a genius," Granny said.

"What? What did I say? Is it really a fish?"

"Not exactly," Uncle Jake said. He cupped his hands around Daphne's ear and whispered something that made the girl's eyes grow as big as Frisbees.

"No way!" Daphne cried as she inserted her palm into her mouth and bit down hard.

The sun had nearly set by the time the girls and their uncle rowed out to the middle of the Hudson River in a tiny boat. When they reached the spot Jake was looking for, he dropped a bright orange anchor overboard.

"The Little Mermaid is the seventh daughter of Poseidon, the ruler of the sea," he said as he fumbled in his pockets. Eventually he took out a small fishing rod. On it was a lure and a hook.

"What kind of magic is that?" Daphne asked.

"It's not magic. It's called a Pocket Fisherman. I bought it on the Internet." Uncle Jake cast his line. "The daughter of the water has to be the Little Mermaid. Giving a piece of the Vorpal blade to her was brilliant on Spaulding's part. Without gills there's no way to get it—unless of course, you're me."

Jack cast the line and Sabrina watched the lure sink beneath the waves.

Every time her uncle mentioned the Little Mermaid by name, Daphne jumped up in excitement, nearly capsizing the boat several times. She'd seen a movie about the character at a friend's house when she was five and afterward spent entire weekends in the bathtub trying to grow fins. Of all the Everafters in the town, Daphne wanted to meet the undersea princess the most.

"I bet we'll become best friends," Daphne said. "She'll invite me over all the time."

"Sure, who wouldn't want to spend all their free time at the bottom of the Hudson River?" Sabrina said. "So, what's the plan? How do we get the Vorpal blade from the mermaid?"

"Just be patient," Uncle Jake said, as he reeled in his line's slack.

After several minutes Sabrina noticed a tugging on the line.

"Looks like I've got a bite," Uncle Jake said, slowly and cautiously reeling in his catch. From the tension in the line, it seemed as if he had hooked a big one. The fish was strong, and a few times Sabrina was sure it would pull Uncle Jake out of the boat. But he was strong, too, and soon he was pulling the fish aboard.

It was huge, probably weighing twenty pounds, with a white belly, gray skin, and a series of purple stripes on either side of its back. It flopped around on the bottom of the boat, smacking against the girls with its tail, and then it did something so shocking that Sabrina nearly fell overboard.

"Jake Grimm!" the fish said in a gurgling voice. "You dirty, filthy, no-good pain in my tail! I should have known when I saw that lure that it was you!"

"How are you doing, Anthony?" Uncle Jake said as he set his rod into the boat. "I wish this could have been avoided, bud, but we need your special talents."

"You're a talking fish," Daphne said.

"You can't get anything past this one," Anthony said. "Are these your kids, Jake? If this brood is the future of the Grimms, I suspect your family is in deep trouble."

"They belong to Henry," Jake explained.

"I heard about his disappearance. Send your mother my best wishes. Now, what do you want?"

"We're going to see the Little Mermaid, and we need to be able to breathe underwater," Uncle Jake explained.

"That's a dumb idea, Jakey!" the fish warned.

"It can't be avoided," Uncle Jake replied. "The mermaid's got something we need."

"She's in a foul mood lately. She's been particularly abusive to her staff. Half of them have been turned into fish sticks. If she kills you, don't come crying to me. I tried to warn you."

"Kills us?" Daphne cried. "That's crazy talk! The Little Mermaid would never kill someone. I know—I saw the movie!"

"She's mean!" Anthony said as he flopped around the boat. "Mean, I tell you!"

"Shut your mouth," Daphne cried. "I don't believe a word you say."

"Your funeral," the fish gurgled. "All right, Jake. I can't refuse a request. You know how this works. Make your wish."

"Wait a minute. You grant wishes?" Sabrina asked.

"I'm a fish that talks, and you're having trouble with me granting wishes?"

"Why are we wishing to be able to breathe underwater? Why don't we just wish we had all the pieces of the Vorpal blade? Why not avoid the headache?" Sabrina asked her uncle.

"Sorry, kid, one wish per customer. I can't grant multipart wishes," the fish said.

"Well, then I wish I had the Little Mermaid's part of the Vorpal blade," Sabrina said.

Just then, a seaweed-covered piece of metal materialized in Sabrina's hands. She picked off the slimy plants and smiled. Its jagged end would fit perfectly with the other piece of the sword.

"All right, Jake," the fish said. "I did my part. Now put me back in the water."

"I really appreciate your help," Uncle Jake said as he scooped the fish up and released him into the river. Anthony drifted back up to the surface and squirted water into Uncle Jake's face.

"Next time, put a worm on that hook. If I'm going to be put out, the least you could do is feed me!" The fish dove under the surface and was gone.

The family examined their treasure with awe.

"You were right, Uncle Jake," Sabrina said. "Magic makes everything easier."

Daphne shrugged. "Granny says there is always a price for using magic."

"Your grandmother just likes to do things the hard way," Uncle Jake said.

Suddenly, there was mighty splash, and a figure sprang out of the water. He was strong, with a barrel chest and big arms. His skin was green-tinged, and he had kelp in his hair. He yanked an orange starfish from a belt around his waist and smacked it onto the top of Daphne's head. He snatched her in his arms and pulled her under the water.

"Daphne!" Sabrina cried, as she searched the surface for her sister.

Sabrina and Uncle Jake desperately called out for the little girl, but there was no reply. Had her sister just been drowned before their eyes? Seconds later there was another splash on the opposite side of the boat. This time, Sabrina got a better look at the man. She noticed, to her shock, that he had a fish tail instead of legs. He slapped another starfish onto Uncle Jake's head and dragged him overboard as well.

Sabrina stuffed the sword piece into one coat pocket, and out of another she took Merlin's wand. She studied the water, examining every ripple and preparing for an attack. When she heard the splash behind her, she spun around, which caused the little boat to dip and roll. She lost her balance, and the wand fell from her hand and rolled to the bottom of the boat. Before she could scramble down to retrieve it, the merman sprang into the boat, nearly capsizing it. He removed a scroll from a little bag on his belt and unfurled it, then cleared his throat and began to read.

"By the order of her majesty, the princess, I do hereby place you and your coconspirators under arrest for acts of thievery," the merman declared.

"You don't understand!" Sabrina argued, but the merman ignored her. He rolled up his scroll and tucked it back into his bag. Then he slapped an orange starfish onto the top of her head. The starfish's five arms clamped down on her skull, acting like suction cups, and suddenly a terrifying sensation came over her. She literally felt like a fish out of water. She couldn't breathe!

8

"W HAT HAVE YOU DONE TO ME?" SABRINA gasped, desperate for air.

"Silence, you filthy, thieving topsider!" the merman barked as he snatched the piece of the Vorpal blade from her pocket. He tucked it under his belt and then grabbed her roughly by the arm. Before Sabrina could struggle, he leaped out of the boat and into the frigid water, taking her with him.

He swam deeper and deeper with Sabrina trapped in his strong grasp. She fought back viciously, punching and kicking her captor, but it didn't seem to faze the merman at all. Soon, her lungs were burning for oxygen. Her mouth instinctively opened, and she inhaled deeply. Icy crystals raced down her throat. A curious heaviness filled her body, and she felt as if water were pouring into her fingers and toes. She closed her eyes, preparing to die, but after several minutes something dawned on her—she could breathe! *It must be the starfish*, she realized.

"Where are you taking me?" Sabrina demanded as a wave of bubbles escaped her mouth. She was surprised to find her voice sounded as normal as it did in air.

The merman said nothing, only pointed to the rapidly approaching river floor, where an incredible sight came into view. Nestled on the rocky bottom of the Hudson River was a city. It had skyscrapers, apartment buildings, and hundreds of mermen and mermaids rushing here and there in the neatly planned grid of streets. From high above, the city was a fantastically beautiful dream of green and aquamarine, but as the merman dragged her closer and closer, the city's secret began to reveal itself. Everything was made out of trash. Entire buildings were made from discarded car tires and license plates. The sidewalks were paved with old bottle caps and the heels of shoes. Homes were constructed from old clothes, wagon wheels, flip-flops, garden tools, computers, antique telephones, grocery carts, beach chairs, cans, bottles, and thousands of tennis balls, footballs, and Frisbees, all stacked with expert care.

The merman pulled Sabrina through the city gates and along a street made of crushed toasters and cast-iron skillets.

"Where did you get all this stuff?" Sabrina asked.

The merman scowled and pointed toward the surface. She looked up, then down again at all the junk. No wonder her captor had so much contempt for her. Every nook and cranny of the odd city owed its existence to two hundred years of junk that people like herself had dumped into the river. Human beings were disgusting.

He turned down one alley and then another. They passed dozens of shops carved out of sunken sailboats—some still had their names painted on the side. Merman and mermaid shop owners stood on the street calling out to passersby, trying to get them to buy old soda bottles and bicycle wheels. A mermother pushed an infant merbaby along the street in an old stroller.

Soon Sabrina and the merman reached an enormous palace, nearly five stories high. From above, Sabrina had thought it was the most beautiful place she had ever seen, but now that she was in front of it she realized it was made of the same junk as the rest of the underwater town. A flight of stairs, which were actually old car bumpers, led to a large door that was guarded by a merman holding a dented trumpet in one hand and a trident in the other.

"I have the last of the topsider prisoners," her captor said.

The merman guard nodded. "You may pass." He swam over and pushed the door open, allowing them to enter a great seaweed-covered hallway. They continued through another doorway, this one unguarded, and down a flight of steps. At the bottom, Sabrina saw several heavy wooden doors with metal bars on their windows. The merman took a set of keys from his belt, opened up the closest door, and shoved Sabrina inside. Daphne and Uncle

Jake sat on a bench in the corner of the room. Daphne looked at her disapprovingly, while Uncle Jake gave her a pitiful smile.

"You will be held here in the dungeon until Her Highness requires your presence," the merman barked. "Then you will be given five minutes to plead your innocence or guilt. Shortly after, you will be executed and your bodies fed to the river's parasites and bottom-feeders."

"What if we're found innocent?" Sabrina asked.

"No one is found innocent," the merman said. He exited the room, slammed the heavy metal door, and locked it tight.

Sabrina turned back to her family. "I dropped the wand in the boat."

"It doesn't matter," Uncle Jake said. "It won't work underwater."

"If I'm fed to bottom-feeders, I will never forgive you!" Daphne said. "You *had* to use magic. Granny said there was always a price, but you wouldn't listen. What are we going to do now?"

"I don't know. We're in big trouble," Uncle Jake said.

Sabrina and Daphne looked at each other. They didn't have to say what they were thinking. In the short time they had known their uncle, he had been Mr. Confidence. If he was giving up already, then the situation was really bad.

"You don't know?" Sabrina said. "You've got an overcoat filled with magic stuff. Start searching your pockets."

"I doubt anything will work. Magic doesn't like getting wet," Uncle Jake said.

"We don't need any of your magic," Daphne said. "I'll do all the talking. I'll tell the princess why we need her part of the sword. She's the Little Mermaid. She's really cool and nice, and she'll totally understand."

"Daphne, this isn't the Little Mermaid from the movies," Uncle Jake explained. "In that movie she fell in love with the prince and was happy, but in the real story, the one Hans Christian Andersen documented, the princess gave up her entire life to be with her prince, and he abandoned her for another woman. He rode off and completely forgot about her. She's never really gotten over it, and she's still a little resentful toward humans. Actually, that's an understatement. She hates humans, especially men. Hell hath no fury like a woman scorned."

"What does *scorned* mean?" Daphne asked her sister.

"It means she got dumped," Sabrina answered, then turned her attention back to her uncle. "So what are we going to do?"

Just then, the door flew open and two hulking merman guards entered. They wore heavy steel helmets and carried silver tridents, which they pointed at the group.

"The princess will see you now!" one of them shouted as he swam over and grabbed Jake. The second brute clamped his big hands on the two girls and dragged them out of the cell. The guards forced the family down the hallway, into a massive, high-ceilinged room, and up to a pair of enormous doors covered in seaweed. An elderly merman with a bushy white beard and spectacles stood nearby at a podium reading a soggy book.

"Yes?" the old merman said without looking up.

"I have the topsiders who stole from the princess," one of the guards said respectfully.

The old merman took off his glasses and squinted as he examined the group. "Yes, yes, let them in!" he shouted. Instantly a school of catfish swam up to the door. Each grabbed on to a strand of seaweed with its mouth, and together they swung the mighty doors open.

The room on the other side was expansive, and though it was constructed out of trash, everything gleamed as if it were made of marble. In the center of the room was the backseat of an old car. It was strung with brilliant white pearls and sat on a pedestal of discarded milk crates. Sabrina thought it resembled a throne, but it hardly seemed regal.

The merman guards escorted the girls and their uncle up to the pedestal and forced them onto their knees.

"Show some respect, ground-walkers!" one of the guards barked.

Just then, a door on the far side of the chamber opened and several mermen swam into the room, carrying dented and broken musical instruments. They blew some bubbly, off-key notes, then a tall, thin merman holding a stone tablet swam forward. "All hail, Poseidon's princess! Her Majesty, the Little Mermaid!"

Sabrina craned her neck to see the princess, but just then an outrageously overweight mermaid swam through the doors and blocked her view. It wasn't until two mermen helped the enormous half woman/half fish onto the throne that Sabrina realized she was indeed looking at the legendary Little Mermaid. It took her assistants several minutes to get the princess into her seat, and then several minutes more for the mermaid to get comfortable. When she was done, she was wheezing like a teakettle. Still, she was beautiful. She had big blue eyes and a mane of gorgeous red hair that flowed down to her fins. She wore a seashell bikini top and an aquamarine sarong. On her head was a pearl-encrusted tiara.

"That's the *Little* Mermaid?" Sabrina said quietly to Uncle Jake.

Uncle Jake nodded. "The breakup was very hard on her. She turned to food for comfort."

The princess picked up a conch shell sitting on the armrest of her throne and blew into it. A low rumbling note filled the air.

"I am hungry. I want a treat," she demanded.

The skinny merman with the tablet approached the throne. "Your Highness, if you will recall, last week you instructed me not to allow you to snack between meals. You told me to kill anyone who offers you anything that isn't on your diet."

"I'm rescinding that order," the princess said. "I want a treat. I've been good all day. I had my seaweed smoothie for breakfast and lunch, and I swam on the treadmill for twenty minutes. I want a treat. I deserve a treat."

"But, Your Majesty . . ."

"*Treat!*" she roared. "*Now!*"

"Very well, Your Highness," the merman said with a worried face. "Bring the princess a treat!"

A second merman soldier shouted, "Bring the princess a treat!" followed by another and another. Soon, the side door flew open and a lowly merman wearing a chef's hat and a white apron swam into the hall with a covered silver platter. He bowed before the princess, took the lid off, and presented a bright pink cake with squiggly tentacles poking out of the sides.

She snatched it from him with greedy fingers.

"It's anemone upside-down cake, your majesty," the chef said nervously. He bowed deeply, left the platter, and hurried off. The princess took a big bite of the odd cake. Sabrina knew her grandmother would die to have the recipe.

"Oh, it's heavenly," the Little Mermaid said with her mouth full. "I think I'll have another tiny bite."

She ate another, and then another, and another, until the whole cake was gone. She looked down at the empty platter and started to cry.

"My lady," the skinny merman said nervously, "what brings you to tears?"

"*I'm fat!*" she cried. "Look at me! I used to be thin! How could you let me eat that cake?"

"But, Your Majesty . . ."

"It's the chef's fault. I want you to feed him to the Cruel Crustacean!"

"But, Your Majesty, he's your favorite chef."

"*Cruel Crustacean!*" she roared. "Now!"

"Feed the chef to the Cruel Crustacean!" the merman assistant shouted. It was quickly repeated throughout the room until a hulking guard ran out the side door with his trident.

"What's the Cruel Crustacean?" Daphne whispered.

Sabrina shrugged. "Uncle Jake, do something."

"What?"

"I don't know. You said you were good with women. You figure it out," Sabrina said.

Uncle Jake smiled. "Your Majesty, I think you're being too hard on yourself. I don't think you're fat. I think you're beautiful."

One of the merman guards stuck his trident dangerously close to Uncle Jake's throat. "*Silence!*" he shouted. "You will not speak until the princess has given you permission."

"Who are these topsiders?" the mermaid asked as she licked the crumbs off her fingers.

"These are the ones who stole your portion of the Vorpal blade," the skinny merman explained to the princess. He set the broken sword on the throne, then backed away.

"Is this true, topsider? Defend yourself!" the Little Mermaid demanded.

"Yes, I stole it," Uncle Jake said. "But the girls had nothing to do with it."

"You are confessing to your crime?" the Little Mermaid asked, surprised. "Most of the topsiders I have met are liars. Why would you admit your guilt and face almost certain death?"

"We need the blade to stop a Jabberwocky that is terrorizing the town," Uncle Jake said.

"Why would that concern me?" the mermaid asked. "Let the monster destroy your town, for all I care. Topsiders deserve no less! You are guilty! Feed them to the Cruel Crustacean!"

The guards seized the Grimms.

"Wait!" Uncle Jake cried. "There was another reason I did it."

"Let him speak," the princess said.

Uncle Jake stammered, but then smiled and said, "I have a crush on you!"

Daphne stepped forward. "It's true. You're all he talks about."

"Twenty-four hours a day," Sabrina added nervously.

"He thinks you're a total hottie!" Daphne added as sincerely as she could. "He wants to marry you and have a million merbabies."

"You're pushing it a bit far," Uncle Jake muttered to the little girl.

"Is this true?" the princess said. Even in the dim underwater light, Sabrina could see her blushing.

"I stole the blade because I wanted to meet you," Uncle Jake explained. "I have been all over the world and have seen a lot of women, but the rumors of your beauty could not be ignored. I had to risk my life to see if those rumors were true."

"Nonsense." The princess giggled. "I've seen the celebrity magazines that float down here from your world. I know I'm not as thin as they are."

"Those women don't hold a candle to you," Uncle Jake replied. "Why, I bet if you came up to the surface you'd be in one of those magazines, too."

"Every word that comes out of your mouth is a filthy lie," the princess snapped. Sabrina gulped. It seemed as if Uncle Jake's plan had fallen apart, until the mermaid's face softened and a wide smile appeared. "And I love every single one of them."

Uncle Jake looked over at Sabrina and winked. Her uncle had his own magic inside him. He was one of the most charming men she had ever met.

"I know what I did was wrong, but I'm glad I did it. Too bad you're going to kill us, though. I would have loved to go back to the surface and tell that ex-boyfriend of yours how gorgeous you still are. He lives in town. I hear he lost all his hair and moved back in with his mom. He's pathetic. He got just what he deserved."

"You say he's miserable?"

"Oh, yes. Just a shell of the man he once was," Uncle Jake replied.

The Little Mermaid smiled. "I wish I could see his face when you tell him how great I am doing."

"I could take a picture and bring it back," Uncle Jake offered.

The princess giggled mischievously. "That's a very tempting offer."

"Since I would be going up there and coming back anyway, you could lend me your portion of the Vorpal blade. Once I'm done with it, I could bring it back to you with the picture, and we could laugh at how stupid your loser ex looks."

The Little Mermaid and Uncle Jake laughed together.

"All right, you naughty boy," the princess said. "You've got yourself a deal. You are free to go, and you can take the blade, too."

"Oh, I knew you would be wonderful!" Daphne said, clapping her hands. "I saw the movie they made about you. It was so romantic!"

Uncle Jake put his hand over the little girl's mouth, but it was too late. The Little Mermaid's face turned red and contorted with anger.

"*Romantic?* Oh, yes, it was romantic. Unfortunately, *it never happened!* There was no 'happily ever after' for me. He dumped me and ran off to marry some tart."

"But he's bald now, princess," Uncle Jake said. "Repugnant. Lives in his parents' basement. Remember?"

"He threw a lot of pretty words around, but he didn't really mean them. He got my hopes up, and then he left me for the first thing with feet that came along. But what should I have expected from a topsider? My parents tried to warn me. My sisters did, too. All topsiders are the same. They're nothing but a bunch of liars."

"Your Majesty. It's obvious you are upset," Sabrina said. "We'll just take the blade and go."

"As I suspected! You're not down here to give me compliments," the overstuffed princess growled. She reached over and seized the Vorpal blade piece from the arm of her throne. "All you want is this! *Feed them to the Cruel Crustacean!*"

The merman guards rushed to a huge wooden wheel that protruded from a nearby wall. Together they struggled to turn it, and as they did, the floor beneath the family disappeared and the Grimms sank into the waters below. They tried to swim back into the throne room, but a dozen vicious-looking merman guards blocked the way. Trapped, the family sank to the sandy floor below and looked around.

"This is bad, right?" Sabrina said, eyeing the dark chamber they found themselves in. "Anything called the Cruel Crustacean can't be looking for a hug."

"Just stay close," Uncle Jake said.

"Look!" Daphne cried as an enormous creature took its first step into the light. It was as big as Granny Relda's house, with eight fat legs that ended in spikes. Its eyes protruded from two long, armlike stalks that wiggled back and forth. It had a massive shell on its back, and when it took a step, the ground beneath the family rumbled. Sabrina recognized the monster for what it was. The Chinese restaurant on the corner near their old apartment in Manhattan had a much smaller one in a tank by the register. It was a hermit crab—a *really* big hermit crab.

"Oh, I'm going to have some really wicked nightmares after this," said Daphne.

Sabrina looked around the chamber. "There's nowhere to hide in here. What are we going to do?"

Uncle Jake took off his overcoat and dropped it at the girls' feet. "I'll fight this thing off as long as I can." He rushed forward, shouting at the ugly beast to distract it from the sisters.

Sabrina snatched her uncle's overcoat and searched through its pockets. "There's got to be something here that will help." She pulled out a red brooch with a black eye painted in the middle. She held it up, and for a brief moment it glowed with power, but then it fizzled out. Sabrina grimaced and shoved it back into the pocket. She found a little black marble hidden in another pocket and threw it at the monster, hoping for some enormous explosion, but it bounced off the hermit crab's shell and was buried in the sand.

"What was that supposed to do?" Daphne asked.

"Beats me! I'm trying everything."

While Sabrina searched, Uncle Jake did his best to stay out of the way of the hermit crab's legs. It was no easy feat. The crab used them as impaling spikes, bringing them down hard and pulverizing the ground. If one of them connected with Uncle Jake, he'd be a goner.

"Let me help," Daphne said as she dug through the overcoat's pockets as well.

"I thought you said magic was bad," Sabrina said.

Daphne scowled at her sister and stuck her tongue out to give her a raspberry.

Together they pulled out a variety of odd-colored rings, carved totems, voodoo dolls, and amulets made from bones. They tried to activate each of the trinkets, but with zero knowledge of what any of them did or how to use them, they failed every time. Nothing was working, and the hermit crab had nearly made a shish kebab of their uncle.

"Look for something that gives you a jolt!" Uncle Jake shouted. "You'll feel the magic if it's going to work down here."

Sabrina dug through more pockets, discarding anything that didn't feel powerful. Finally, she reached into a pocket and it felt as if something had given her an electrical shock.

"What are these?" Sabrina asked, yanking out a pair of slippers.

"The Shoes of Swiftness!" Uncle Jake shouted. "Put them on!"

Sabrina examined the slippers closely. "What do they do?"

Uncle Jake was too busy with the crab to answer, so Sabrina kicked off her shoes and pulled on the slippers. She immediately felt an energy, much like the one Merlin's wand had given her. It was incredible and powerful.

Just then, Uncle Jake cried out in pain. Sabrina spun around and found him up against a wall with nowhere to run and the crab raising a deadly spike to skewer him. There was no escape for him.

"No!" Sabrina said, instinctively running to his side, and as she did, something marvelous happened. Her feet moved so fast she was able to snatch her uncle out of the way of certain death. In a flash she and her uncle were standing next to a dumbfounded Daphne.

"OK, that was cool," Daphne admitted.

"I've got an idea," Sabrina said, staring up at the hole. "Grab on to my arms and hold on tight!"

Daphne slipped her hand into her sister's. Uncle Jake reached down, grabbed his overcoat, and then slipped his free hand into Sabrina's. The Cruel Crustacean charged at them, but in the blink of an eye they were gone. Sabrina's legs became a blur, and in no time the three of them were propelled upward as if they were attached to a powerboat motor. They rocketed to freedom through the hole, shocking the merman guards. Sabrina spotted the Vorpal blade, still in the chubby hands of the mermaid princess, and darted in her direction. As they passed her, Uncle Jake snatched it away.

"Thanks, beautiful," he quipped.

The Little Mermaid screamed with rage, and a gurgling alarm was sounded. A second later, Sabrina watched as the massive doors to the chamber began to close.

"They're trying to trap us inside!" Uncle Jake warned.

"Hang on!" Sabrina cried, and started kicking, this time aiming for the narrowing gap between the doors. Again they rocketed forward, just slipping through before the doors crushed them to death. They streaked across the main hall, out through the gate, and into the busy streets. Kicking as hard as she could, Sabrina propelled the family down the road, sending mermen and mermaids leaping out of their path. Once they were safely away from the palace, Sabrina angled toward the surface of the river.

"Any idea where the boat is?" she asked.

"Over there!" Daphne said, pointing to the bright orange anchor they had tossed over the side.

"I recommend we get there as fast as we can," Uncle Jake said, pointing below. Sabrina looked down and saw an army of angry merman guards swimming toward them. Following on their heels was the enormous hermit crab.

Sabrina kicked faster toward the surface. Unfortunately, she misjudged the power of her feet, and the group exploded out of the water, flying fifteen feet into the air. A moment later they came crashing back down into the river. Uncle Jake was the first to struggle to the surface again. He pulled Daphne and Sabrina over to the boat, and they all climbed in. Uncle Jake snatched up the oars and rowed furiously, but they'd forgotten to pull up the anchor; it held them in place.

"I can't breathe!" Daphne cried suddenly. Uncle Jake dropped the oars and yanked the sticky starfish off the little girl's head with a *slurp!* Daphne gasped at first, but soon she was breathing fine and helped Sabrina pull off her own starfish. Uncle Jake shoved his into his overcoat.

"Might come in handy someday," he said, as he began to pull up the heavy anchor.

The first wave of merman soldiers leaped out of the water like dolphins, flapping their tails back and forth to stay above the surface. They were several yards away from the boat but held their tridents menacingly as they approached the family. A second wave of soldiers appeared behind them, followed by the rising shell of the giant hermit crab. It opened its ugly mouth, and a high-pitched scream erupted from its throat. When the first trident struck the side of the boat, Sabrina knew they had to do something, and fast. She leaped to her feet, snatched a length of the anchor rope, and moved to the stern.

"What are you doing?" Uncle Jake asked as he finally dragged the anchor out of the water.

"I have absolutely no idea," Sabrina said, and she took off toward the bow of the boat and leaped onto the water. Her legs were going a mile a minute, so fast she couldn't even see her own feet. Each step was so quick that she found she could run on top of the water as if it were pavement. She raced across the surface of the Hudson River toward the shore. With the rope in hand she dragged the boat behind her, leaving a powerful wake that built up strength and slammed into the merman army like a tidal wave.

When she reached the shore, she was so excited that she kept on running up the embankment, across some train tracks—narrowly missing the express to Grand Central Terminal—and into the forest, where she finally came to a stop. Her feet felt like they were on fire. She kicked the magic slippers off as quickly as she could. The energy that they had given her quickly faded, and she wanted to put them back on, even though she knew they would burn her feet. She was about to actually do it when Uncle Jake handed her Merlin's wand.

"I found this in the bottom of the boat," he said.

Sabrina snatched it away, surprised by how greedy she was for it. The magic swirled through her, and she smiled. Daphne gave her a startled, disapproving look, but Sabrina ignored it.

"Well, that's two out of three," Uncle Jake said, holding up the piece of the broken sword. He looked down at the inscription on it.

Beg the hag of the hills, it read.

Sabrina dipped a washcloth into the bowl of cool water that sat next to Puck's bed and wrung it out. Then she patted it across the boy's fevered brow. He mumbled incoherently for a few moments and then went back to sleep.

Granny and Uncle Jake were in the living room, busily searching the journals for references to a "hag of the hills," while Daphne had long since surrendered to sleep and was napping in a rocking chair next to the bed. It was late, and though Sabrina knew a cup of coffee would keep her awake, the bitter taste wasn't worth it. Instead, she found that by lightly touching Merlin's wand in her pocket, she got enough of a jolt of energy to completely refresh her. She wanted to look after Puck in case he woke and needed something.

A wave of emotions overtook her, emotions she didn't understand: genuine concern for the boy, anger at his recklessness, confusion at the memory of their kiss. She felt like crying when she remembered how vicious her rejection of him had been.

"Hey, stink-bottom," Sabrina said, wondering if the boy could hear her. If he could, he'd never let her live down any kind words she might say to him. Besides, trading insults with her seemed to be his favorite game. Maybe it would make him feel better deep down. "You realize you're a terrible burden on all of us. Look at yourself lying in that bed. You're not fooling anyone. I'd bet a hundred bucks that you're faking all of this just for the attention. Well, your pampering is about to come to an end, buster. When we have all the pieces of the Vorpal blade, we're going to find the Blue Fairy and put them back together. Once we kill the Jabberwocky, Red Riding Hood will be no problem. Mom and Dad will come home, and then we're shipping you off to the fairy folk. You'll be back to being a pain in my butt in no time at all."

She looked over at her sister to make sure she was still sleeping, and then removed the wand from her pocket. She laid it on the bed and examined it with awe. Just having it near made her feel like everything was going to be fine. She could handle everything herself. Puck would live, and she'd bring her parents home. Nothing could get in her way.

"Are you OK?" Daphne asked.

"I'm fine," Sabrina said, snatching the wand off the bed and stuffing it back into her pocket.

"You were staring at that thing for fifteen minutes," Daphne said. "I said your name a few times, but you didn't hear me."

Sabrina shot a glance at the clock on the wall. Her sister was right. "I have a lot on my mind."

"I want you to give that thing to Granny," Daphne insisted. "It belongs in the mirror, where it will be safe."

"It'll be safe with me."

Daphne got out of her chair and crossed the room. She stood over Sabrina and looked at her closely. "But are you going to be safe from it?"

"You're being silly."

"No, I'm not," the little girl said, a bit too loudly. "I saw your face when you used the wand. It was the same face you made when you used the shoes."

"What face is that?"

"You looked like you wanted to hurt someone," Daphne said.

"No, what I looked like was someone who wasn't afraid anymore," Sabrina said. "Daphne, aren't you sick to death of running all the time?"

"The first thing I learned in Ms. White's self-defense class was that there are things that you stand and fight and there are things that you run from. A smart warrior knows the difference. You used to know the difference."

"You know, when I woke up in the hospital you claimed that I didn't include you in things anymore," Sabrina complained. "Did you ever think it was because everything I do is wrong in your eyes?"

"We are still a team," Daphne said. "And you are still wrong. You're getting add . . . add . . . what's that word Granny said earlier?"

"Addicted?"

"Yes, addicted."

"Whatever."

"Don't you 'whatever' me!"

They sat in silence, and eventually Daphne said, "I'm going to bed."

"Fine," Sabrina said, still angry about her sister's accusation.

"Be careful, Sabrina," Daphne whispered, and she stepped out of the room.

A loud, raspy breath woke Sabrina from her sleep. The room was dark, and a girlish giggle sent Sabrina dashing to the light switch. She flipped it on and realized at once that she wasn't in her grandmother's room anymore. She was in her own bed, and standing by it was the Jabberwocky and Red Riding Hood. Sabrina reached into her pocket and took out Merlin's wand. She aimed it at the monster and thought about big bolts of lightning rocking the sky.

"How did you get in here?" she asked.

The little girl laughed. "Silly."

"Where are my parents?" Sabrina demanded, eyeing Daphne.

She was sound asleep and snoring heavily. Daphne could sleep through a war.

"They're safe. I've got my grandmother now and my doggy."

"You lie!"

The little girl giggled.

"*Granny!*" Sabrina shouted, but the old woman didn't reply. "*Mr. Canis!*" There was no sound.

"All I need is one more member of my family before we can play house. I need a little sister," Red Riding Hood said. Sabrina gasped, and the Jabberwocky took a step toward Daphne's slumbering body.

"No!" Sabrina cried, and a flash of light exploded through the window. It hit the Jabberwocky in the back and knocked it to its knees.

"Stop!" Red Riding Hood cried. "You'll kill my kitty!"

Sabrina didn't care. She shot another bolt to hit the downed beast. It screeched in pain. Dozens more blasts lit up the room. The Jabberwocky cried out as each one fried it with white-hot light. To Sabrina, the cries sounded like pleas for mercy, but she wouldn't listen. She wanted this thing dead, and soon she got her wish. The monster slumped to the ground, gasped, and was still.

Red Riding Hood rushed to the Jabberwocky's body and cried in despair. "You killed her!"

Sabrina smiled in triumph. She walked over to get a better

view, but she was surprised to find that the monster was no longer there. Its massive, smoldering carcass had been replaced with the body of young girl with blond hair. Stunned, Sabrina dropped to her knees to see the girl's face. She brushed away the hair and gasped. "It's me!"

Sabrina turned to the mirror in her room and nearly screamed when she saw her reflection. Her legs were gone, replaced with hulking clawed feet. She looked down at them and noticed that she also had a long reptilian tail. It swung around the room uncontrollably, destroying the little desk and dresser. Her arms had become a scaly mass of muscles and tendons with razor-sharp talons on her fingertips. She screamed for someone to help her, but no one came. She was turning into the Jabberwocky. She was becoming a monster, and no one could help.

"They tried to warn you," Red Riding Hood said. She laughed maniacally as she put a huge leash around Sabrina's neck. "Come on, kitty. Let's play."

"Sabrina!" a voice shouted. She felt someone's hand gently shaking her shoulder. She looked over and saw Granny Relda's concerned face.

"You were having a nightmare," she said.

Sabrina looked down at her body. It was back to normal. She had had another of her awful dreams.

"Are you OK?" her grandmother asked.

Sabrina nodded.

"Well, put on something warm. Your uncle and I have discovered who the hag of the hills is," Granny Relda said.

"Good! Where's Uncle Jake?" Sabrina asked as she got up.

"He's downstairs having a drink," the old woman said.

"A drink? Why?"

"To calm his nerves, I suppose. He's not too excited about who has the last piece of the Vorpal blade."

"I don't understand," Sabrina said. "Who's got the last piece?"

"The witch," Granny said. "The one called Baba Yaga."

9

SABRINA HAD HEARD MANY STORIES ABOUT
Baba Yaga and read even more. What she knew was disturbing. Baba Yaga was thousands of years old, and it
was rumored that she was a cannibal. Many of the family journals
described heart-stopping encounters with her. They talked of her
home, decorated with the bones of her latest meal. She seemed
like an odd ally for the Grimm family, but time and time again the
family had turned to her for help.

Baba Yaga was responsible for the barrier that kept the Everafters in Ferryport Landing. But nothing she did came without a
price. As payment for the spell, Baba Yaga had stolen the Grimm
family's freedom forever: a Grimm would have to stay in the town
as long as the barrier existed.

"So she eats people?" Daphne whispered to her sister in the
backseat of the car as they drove to see the witch. Her arms were

wrapped around Elvis as if he were a life preserver and she were lost at sea.

Sabrina nodded. "That's the story."

"That's so gross," Daphne said. She hugged the Great Dane. "Don't let anybody eat me, Elvis."

Elvis whined, then turned his attention to the paper sack Granny had given them for the trip. Granny had stayed behind with Puck but said the girls would need whatever was inside to get to the witch. It was like a magnet to the big dog's nose.

Uncle Jake was silent and pale as he drove the car along the road that snaked across Mount Taurus. The girls tried to ask him more about the witch. After all, he had come face to face with her and survived, but he seemed to be in a different world. Sabrina reached into her pocket and clutched Merlin's wand. The little charge she felt racing through her body gave her courage.

We'll be just fine, she told herself. *And if we aren't, that old crone is going to regret it.*

Uncle Jake pulled over to the side of the road and parked the car.

"Why are we stopping?" Sabrina glanced out the window at the dense, snow-covered forest. The trees lining the road looked black, even in the morning sunlight, as if their life force had been stolen.

"We're here," Uncle Jake replied. He looked out the car window into the woods and cracked his knuckles nervously.

Daphne peered in every direction. "Where's here?"

"You two stay in the car. I'll be right back."

"What?" the girls cried.

"I'll be back soon," he promised.

"No way!" Sabrina protested. "We're going with you."

"It's too dangerous," Uncle Jake cried. "Trust me, girls. If I didn't have to go, I wouldn't. The last time I ran into Baba Yaga, she told me she'd skin me and eat me as jerky. It's best if you wait in the car."

"I can't believe you!" Sabrina complained. "After the lecture you gave Granny about how she was holding us back, now you're treating us like a couple of little kids, too!"

"Uh, we are a couple of little kids," Daphne said.

Sabrina ignored her. "We've seen bigger trouble than this Baba Yaga lady. We killed a giant. We stopped Rumpelstiltskin. Why, a couple of hours ago I rescued us all from a hermit crab as big as a house. We're going."

Sabrina opened the door, got out of the car, and turned to her sister. "Come on."

"Fine, but if she turns us into jerky, I'm telling Granny," the little girl grumbled. She got out of the car and pulled Elvis along with her.

"Just stay close, then," Uncle Jake said.

"Wait! The bag!" Daphne said. She reached through the

window and grabbed Granny's paper sack, then rejoined the group.

Elvis led the way deeper and deeper into the forest, through glades that were deadly quiet. The trees were closely packed, as if huddling together might save them from something. Sabrina could feel an odd creepiness around her. At times, she was sure they were being watched. Every twig that snapped or bird that whistled caused Uncle Jake to jump. Luckily, just a brush of her hand against the magic wand in her pocket gave Sabrina the strength to keep going.

Soon they found a path made of white oval stones that stuck up from the ground at different angles, making it difficult to walk. Daphne quickly lost her footing and fell to her knees. As Sabrina helped her up, the little girl screamed.

"W-w-what?" Uncle Jake stammered.

"Look!" Daphne cried, as she pointed down at the path.

Sabrina bent over and brushed some snow off one of the stones, and her heart stopped. The path wasn't made of stones at all. It was a collection of human skulls, all looking up at them with horrible death grins.

"Gross!" Daphne shouted.

"At least we know we're getting close," Sabrina said.

"That's what they all thought, too!" Uncle Jake said. Sabrina noticed he was sweating even in the frigid winter air.

Just then, a bright orange cat appeared. It stood on the path hissing and baring its fangs. Elvis growled menacingly at it, but the cat was not impressed.

"Let's go back," Uncle Jake said.

"What? Why?" Sabrina said. "It's a cat!"

"It's not a cat," her uncle insisted.

"Come on, stop being silly," Sabrina said, and walked toward the angry feline. Much to her surprise, the creature changed with every step she took toward it until it was a troubling mix of tiger and man that stood as tall as her uncle. Sabrina reached for her wand, but before she could remove it and attack, Daphne and her uncle rushed over and yanked her back. With every step backward the creature morphed back into the cat.

"OK, you were right. It's not a cat," Sabrina said.

"His name is Bright Sun," Uncle Jake said. "He's one of Baba Yaga's bodyguards."

"What kind of witch has bodyguards?" Sabrina asked.

Suddenly, there was a low growl behind them. The group spun around and found a little black terrier on the path behind them. A high-pitched shriek from above sent their gaze upward to a red-tailed hawk landing on a tree limb over their heads.

"We're being attacked by a pet store," Sabrina grumbled.

"The dog is Black Midnight, and the bird is Red Dawn. They expect an offering before we can pass."

Sabrina pulled the wand out of her pocket. "Well, _
solution to this problem."

"Uh, hello?" Daphne said as she shook the paper sack. "Granny
gave us this for a reason. Maybe there's something in here that can
help that doesn't require you to blow anything up."

The little girl opened the sack and her face curled up in revulsion. She reached inside and took out a small brown mouse. It
was dead. Daphne tossed it to the ground, and the hawk swooped
down and snatched it in its sharp talons. Daphne reached into the
sack again and pulled out a can of sardines. She turned the key
and rolled back the lid, then set the can on the ground. Bright
Sun bounded toward it and ate the little fish hungrily. Finally,
she took a small rubber bone from the bag. She squeezed it, and
it squeaked. She tossed the bone to the terrier, who caught it in
his mouth and chewed happily. Then, without a sound, the three
animals stepped off the path.

"Looks like Granny is right," Daphne said. "You don't need
magic to solve everything."

Sabrina shrugged and put the wand back in her pocket, and the
family continued farther down the path.

They came to a clearing where a tiny one-story shack sat at the
end of the skull path. From afar, its little white fence made the
house look quaint, as if it were an abandoned summer cottage in
need of a bit of tender loving care. But as Sabrina got closer she

got another jolt of surprise. The fence was actually made from bleached human bones. The yard was full of broken cauldrons and animal skeletons, including the skull of a catlike animal with massive tusks. The house had a heavy wooden door on the front and two little windows that looked like eyes staring down at them.

Sabrina opened the gate, stepped into the yard, and walked to the front door. A wind chime on the fence clinked as it caught a soft breeze. She examined the chimes. They were made from dried ears and rusty screws. She cringed. "Don't look," she said.

"We won't," Daphne and Uncle Jake replied from far off.

Sabrina turned to see her little sister, her uncle, and Elvis still cowering at the gate. "Come on!" she said. "Don't be a bunch of chickens."

"I've got a bad feeling about this," Daphne said as she and the rest of the group took a hesitant step into the yard.

Sabrina knocked on the heavy door, but there was no reply. She knocked again with the same results.

"She's not home. Let's come back later," Daphne said.

"That's ridiculous. Where do you think she's gone? She's a witch," Sabrina argued.

"Maybe she's at the witch grocery store. I don't know," Daphne said testily.

"There's no such thing as a witch grocery store," Sabrina snapped. Her little sister was getting on her nerves.

"*Girls!*" Uncle Jake shouted. "Let's just go in and get this over with before she gets back. We'll search for the sword and count our blessings that we didn't have to see her."

Sabrina pushed on the door and stepped inside. Immediately she felt her body tingling, as if there were a million wands in her pocket. Magic was all around her, swirling through her fingers and hair, tickling her toes, wrapping around her body like a hug.

The room was dim, and the only light source was a crackling fire burning in a fireplace in the next room. Still, Sabrina could see the place was packed with unusual items; old jars and buckets of icky black goop, a table littered with ancient books, and odd, bubbling potions that popped and hissed. Everything was filthy. The floor was thick with dust. A crud-covered chandelier hung from the ceiling. Rotten apples rested on the fireplace mantel, and the smell burned Sabrina's nose.

She stepped over to a table and picked up one of the enormous books. She opened it and found the scrawls of a shaky hand, recording mysterious incantations in both English and a language she had never seen before. Something inside her wanted to speak the words out loud. She was sure something amazing would happen. She flipped through more pages and realized the paper felt odd under her fingertips. It was almost alive. She peered at it closely in the flickering light and realized little hairs were sticking out of it. It was made from human skin! She dropped the book and took a step backward, only to feel a blast of intense heat from the fireplace behind her. She spun around and saw flames reaching out to her. She could have sworn there were faces in the fire—faces crying out for mercy and freedom.

Suddenly, there was a horrible scream. It came from behind the door of a neighboring room. Everyone froze. Uncle Jake looked like he was going to be sick, but somehow they managed to find the courage to creep along to find the source of the sound. Taking a deep breath, Sabrina pushed the door open and stepped inside.

There was Baba Yaga sitting in a broken rocking chair. Her hair was dry and gray, and a great deal of it stuck out of a wart on her long, pointy nose. Her fingernails were nearly as long as her arms, and her face was wrinkled and scarred. One of her eyes was milky white, and it seemed to look in a different direction than the other, and her teeth—oh, her teeth were the worst! They were so sharp that she must have filed them into points.

And she was watching TV.

"I'm sorry. I didn't hear you knock," she said in a thick Russian accent. She grinned and gestured to the screen. "I get so caught up in my soaps. Hope just caught Bo having an affair with Marlena. You should have heard her scream. It was hilarious. But that's what Hope gets. She was cheating on Bo with John when they went to Spain. Now's not the time to get on a moral high horse."

The family stared at the witch, dumbfounded.

"You don't watch *Days of Our Lives*?" she asked.

Everyone shook their heads.

"Oh, well," the witch said as she was magically lifted out of the chair and placed on the floor by an unseen force. "Relda said you were coming to ask the Old Mother for a favor. I do so enjoy a good barter."

"So, you're not going to eat us?" Daphne said.

Baba Yaga looked the girls over from head to toe. "Children are mostly gristle. Jacob, on the other hand, is another story. I believe I promised to feast on your innards the next time I saw your face."

Uncle Jake shuddered. "I w-w-wouldn't have come if it w-w-wasn't important," he stammered. "We need your part of the Vorpal blade."

"Is that the favor?" she cried, then burst into giggles that quickly turned into a coughing fit. "Spaulding Grimm brought me the blade. He told me never to give it to anyone . . . What's the matter, Jacob? Do I make you nervous?"

Sabrina clutched the wand in her pocket and stepped forward bravely.

"We don't have time for this. Are you going to give us the blade or not?" she demanded.

"A favor comes at a price," the witch said.

"What do you want?" Sabrina asked, reaching into her other pocket. She pulled out a couple dollars in change. She urged her sister to do the same. Daphne managed to produce a little rubber ball, a button, a paper clip, and ten cents. "I suppose if this isn't enough, we could mow your lawn in the summertime, maybe dust your bones and headstones."

"I want the wand," Baba Yaga said, locking her eyes on Sabrina.

The words felt like a slap in the face. For the last few days, Sabrina had felt confident like never before, and it was all due to Merlin's wand. When it was in her hand, she no longer had to run. Bad guys backed away. It gave her a strength she'd always wanted. Asking her to give it up was like asking her to hand over a leg or an arm.

"I don't know what you're talking about," she lied.

The witch smiled broadly, revealing a mouth full of puffy gums. "The child has been touched, Jacob," she said, eyeing the man. "Just like her uncle."

"No, she hasn't," Uncle Jake growled, as he turned to Sabrina. "Give it to her, 'Brina."

"No," Sabrina said, backing away. "We might need it when we face Red Riding Hood and the Jabberwocky."

"Then there will be no favor," Baba Yaga said. "Now go away! *Judge Judy* is on in ten minutes, and I don't want to miss it."

"Sabrina, give it to her," Daphne said.

With her little sister and uncle staring her down, she took the wand out of her pocket. She intended to hand it over, but the jolt of magic it gave her completely changed her mind. She couldn't give it away. She would never let it go. She pointed it at the old woman. Her hand was shaking with anger. "Then we'll take the blade from you!"

The witch cocked an eyebrow at her and sneered. "You don't want me as your enemy, child."

"You can't have it!"

Suddenly, Uncle Jake reached into his pocket and removed a small fire-red stone. Energy emanated from it and illuminated the room. A shocking force yanked the wand out of Sabrina's hands and sent it sailing across the room and into Baba Yaga's hand. Sabrina's courage was replaced with rage at her uncle for betraying her.

"OK, Old Mother," Uncle Jake said. "You've got your payment. Let's see the merchandise."

"Very well," the witch said as she stepped across the room to a table. An old mug that read FOXY GRANDMA sat on top. It was overflowing with wands, and she carelessly stuffed Merlin's in with the others. She opened a drawer in the table; inside was a shiny piece of metal that, unlike the other portions of the blade, had no inscription carved into it. There were no clues to the whereabouts of the Blue Fairy.

"Rumor has it that the Blue Fairy is the only one in this town powerful enough to connect this piece with the others," Uncle

Jake said. "If the price was right, could you share her address with us?"

The old crone shook her head, causing mounds of hair to fall from her head and onto the floor.

"You push your luck, Jacob. Your mother saved you from my hungry teeth this time. You should go home and thank her. Next time, her kindness will not prevent me from sucking the marrow out of your bones."

Uncle Jake's face turned white. Elvis let out a surprised yelp.

"Tell Relda I said hello," Baba Yaga continued, then clapped her hands. Red Dawn, Bright Sun, and Dark Midnight entered the room. "My knights will escort you out of my forest."

Jake nodded to her respectfully and without another word led the girls toward the door, following the witch's beastly bodyguards outside and down the path.

"Well, that went better than I expected," Uncle Jake said. "I got to live, and we got the last piece of the blade!"

Daphne hugged Elvis tightly. "You were so brave!"

"Let's get this home and see what Mom has to say about it," Uncle Jake said.

"No," Sabrina said, stopping and stomping her foot. "I can't leave the wand with her. It belongs to me, and we need it. She doesn't even care that she has it. She tossed it aside like it was nothing. Well, it's not nothing! That wand might save our lives."

"Sabrina, get ahold of yourself," Uncle Jake snapped. "We got what we came for, and we will live to tell about it. Forget the wand. It's gone."

Caught up in a fury she had never expected, Sabrina reached into her uncle's overcoat pocket and snatched the Shoes of Swiftness. They were on her feet before anyone could stop her. "I'm going back for it! She won't even know I was in there."

"Sabrina, no!" Uncle Jake cried, but it was too late.

Sabrina zoomed back to the house and opened the door, and in a flash she was racing into Baba Yaga's room. She snatched the mug off the little table at a speed faster than the human eye could follow, and turned to exit just as fast. Unfortunately, Baba Yaga stuck out a bony leg and tripped her, causing Sabrina to slam hard onto the floor. The little mug of wands fell off the table and shattered, spraying the magical devices in every direction.

"Your grandmother would be disappointed to know you are a thief," the witch said. "Cooking you would save her the anguish of finding out."

Sabrina searched through the scattered collection of wands. There were so many, and Baba Yaga was closing on her fast. She managed to snatch one before she felt herself yanked off her feet by her hair. The witch was inhumanly strong, and Sabrina dangled in front of her.

The witch cackled. "I'll give you some credit. You're braver than your uncle. He snuck in here and ran like a rat when I found him. You're still putting up a fight. Sadly, your passion is fueled by your addiction. It's made you so blind you can't even tell that you're not holding Merlin's wand. All that one does is turn people into frogs."

"Well, then I hope you like flies, ugly," Sabrina said as she conjured a big, fat, slimy frog in her mind. There was a sudden zap and a cloud of dust.

"You really have to be sure to point those things in the right direction," the witch said as the air cleared. Sabrina found she was no longer in the witch's grasp; in fact, she was staring directly at the woman's crusty, corny feet.

Fudge, I made her a giant, Sabrina thought to herself as Baba Yaga's gnarled hand reached down and scooped her off the floor.

"Oh, goodie for me," the witch said as she held Sabrina close to her face. "I haven't had frog legs since the last time I was in Paris."

Frog legs? What is she talking about? Sabrina looked down at herself. Her feet were green and webbed. Her skin was slimy and sticky. Her belly was a massive sac hanging between two skinny legs. A bubbling gurgle churned in her gut, slowly rising up through her body, and then her wide mouth opened. "I'm a frog!" she croaked.

Baba Yaga slowly dipped Sabrina down into her open jaws. Sabrina struggled and used her webbed feet to block her descent into the witch's hungry mouth. Wiggling frantically, she managed to pop out of the witch's grasp and tumbled to the floor. Without allowing herself any time to recover, she leaped toward the door, flailing and screaming as she went. Her new amphibious body could jump incredible lengths, but controlling the leaps was impossible.

"My lunch!" the witch cried. "She's getting away! Red Dawn, Bright Sun, Dark Midnight . . . help Mommy!"

The animals raced into the room and chased after Sabrina. She hopped as fast as she could, and her springlike legs propelled her to greater heights, but she just barely avoided the creatures' sharp claws and vicious fangs. She bounded into the next room and spotted the front door on the opposite wall. One mighty leap sent her flying face first into it, and she fell, dazed and hurt, as the witch's guardians rushed toward her. All three grew and changed. Bright Sun returned to his tiger-warrior form, while Red Dawn morphed into a horrible birdlike man with a savage beak and rippling arms. Black Midnight's transformation was equally disturbing. When it was finished, he was a hunched, muscled giant with thick black hair all over his body and savage fangs. They all wore armor and held long swords in their hands.

Sabrina bounced onto the table that held the witch's potions and powders. She knocked over vials and bowls while the three guardians swung their swords at her frog body. They destroyed ancient books and scrolls with each mighty blow. Sabrina managed to keep ahead of them, but she knew she couldn't outrace them forever.

Bright Sun landed a blow that nearly took off her webbed foot and upended a bowl, splattering himself with a particularly foul-smelling potion. Whatever had been in the bowl instantly transformed him into a little red mouse, and he scurried across the floor, drawing the attention of Red Dawn. The hawk-man dove for the mouse, only to miss and knock over a vial of blue powder than turned him into a tiny spider. Black Midnight kept up the chase, but quickly suffered a fate similar to his companions. Something spilled on him that made his body inflate like a balloon, and he drifted to the ceiling where he was unable to get down.

Sabrina leaped to the floor and headed for the front door. She soon realized that without hands to open it she was trapped.

"Uncle Jake!" she cried. "Open the door!"

The door swung open, and Sabrina hopped out into the cold air. Her family stared down at her with mouths agape.

"All right, let me say it for you: 'I told you so!'" Sabrina grumbled.

"Is that you?" Uncle Jake asked, reaching down and picking her up off the ground.

"Yes," she said. "You're squeezing too hard."

Just then, a window opened and the witch stuck her head out of it. She shook her fist at the family and screamed.

"She's mine. She tried to steal from me!"

"You know I can't give her back, Old Mother," Uncle Jake said.

"I was hoping you'd say that," the witch said, followed by a liquid cackle that bubbled up her throat. When she was done, the ground started to shake.

"What's going on?" Daphne asked.

"Here, hold your sister," Uncle Jake said, as he put Sabrina into Daphne's hands. He nervously picked through his pockets, yanking out odds and ends and growing more discouraged by the second.

"What's going on?" Sabrina asked, struggling for a view around Daphne's thumb. Uncle Jake turned to her and tried to explain, but his words were drowned out by a horrible tearing sound. Sabrina couldn't believe her eyes, even after all that she'd just experienced, but Baba Yaga's house lifted itself off the ground on two massive chicken legs. It walked toward them, scratching at the earth with its terrible talons. Sabrina would have screamed, but all that came out was "Ribbit!" Daphne and Elvis both whined at the same time.

"You know what? Let's just make a run for it!" Uncle Jake said. He spun around, snatched Daphne's free hand, and dragged her back down the path. Elvis followed, barking and growling at the house that stomped after them.

"I hope you're happy," Daphne said to Sabrina. "When we find Mom and Dad, I'm telling!"

The thick forest slowed the house down a little, but with each step its sharp chicken claws got closer and closer, eventually snagging the back of Uncle Jake's overcoat. Desperate, he slipped out of the coat and left it behind.

Distracted, the house stopped abruptly and lowered itself to the ground. Baba Yaga popped out of the front door, scurried over to the overcoat, and snatched it up in her gnarled hands. She rifled through the pockets and let out a laugh that echoed through the woods. Sabrina turned her little frog head and saw Baba Yaga holding the final piece of the sword high in the air above her head. Her heart sank. They'd been so close to recovering the third piece of the blade, and she'd ruined it. Why couldn't she have just let the old woman have the wand? Why had she been so reckless?

But then the witch did something incredible. She tossed the blade through the air. It landed at Uncle Jake's feet. "You forgot your prize, Jacob!" she shouted, then held up his overcoat. "I'll take this as payment for the child's thieving ways."

She rolled it into a ball and went back into her house. The gigantic chicken legs lifted it once again. Awkwardly, it turned itself around, then lumbered back the way it had come.

"Uncle Jake, I'm so sorry," Sabrina said. "It's my fault you lost all your magic."

"What's important is we have the last piece of the blade," Daphne said. "Uncle Jake can find a new coat."

"Except I did have a magic potion in my inside pocket we could have used to de-frog Sabrina," their uncle said.

"What am I going to do?" Sabrina groaned.

"I think you should stay like that for a while and think about how you're behaving," Daphne said.

"I absolutely agree," a voice said from nearby. The group turned and found Mr. Canis lurking in the trees.

"Mom sent you to check up on us, huh?" Uncle Jake said, sounding offended.

Canis ignored the question. He approached the group and stared down at Sabrina, who was still resting in her sister's hands.

"How did you get into this situation?" he said.

"She had a run-in with Baba Yaga," Daphne said.

Sabrina looked up at her and flashed an angry look with her big frog eyes.

"A run-in?" he pressed.

"She took something of mine, and I wanted it back. A wand, a magic wand," Sabrina croaked.

"And how did you come across a magic wand?" Mr. Canis growled, studying Uncle Jake.

"Uh, I gave it to her," Uncle Jake admitted.

The old man's eyes glowed with anger. "The child is eleven years old. Full-grown adults can't handle that kind of magic."

"I was trying to prepare them for the future," Jake said.

"She looks prepared, Jacob," Mr. Canis barked. "Do you have a way to change her back?"

"I was going to take her home. Mom is sure to have something in the Hall of Wonders that will fix her," Uncle Jake said.

Mr. Canis grabbed him roughly by the collar. "You expect your mother to clean up every mess you make!"

"It's a simple changing spell!" Uncle Jake cried. "She's not hurt."

"I'm not talking about the spell! Sabrina risked her life and the safety of her family for a stupid magic trinket. She is clearly touched, and her addiction is your fault!"

"Mr. Canis," Daphne said setting her hand on his arm. "It's OK."

The child's comforting words had a soothing effect on the old man, and he let Uncle Jake go.

"I can tell you now there is nothing in the mirror that can make this right. The spell has only one remedy—the kiss of someone with royal blood."

"Perfect—Puck claims to be royalty," Uncle Jake said, visibly cheered.

Sabrina wondered if anyone could tell when a frog blushed. She hoped not.

"Puck is still very ill," Mr. Canis said.

"Well, this town is crawling with princes," Uncle Jake said. "Who should we call?"

"Unfortunately, you're forcing me to ask a favor of my bitterest enemy," the old man growled.

"You don't mean Prince Charming?" Daphne cried.

"Absolutely not!" Sabrina shouted.

"*Absolutely not!*" Mayor Charming bellowed.

"It's the only way," Mr. Canis said.

Charming's eyes searched his mansion as if he were looking for an escape route. The entire house was doubling as his campaign headquarters, and signs blocked most of the windows. There was no place to run or hide. When he realized he was stuck, he scowled. "The Big Bad Wolf is asking for my help? The devil must have his long underwear on today."

The two stared at each other in disgust. They had a long history, and none of it was nice. Most of the time when the two got together, Granny Relda had to separate them like schoolboys bent on fist fighting.

"You can do it on your own, or you can do it with a substantial bite taken out of you," Mr. Canis threatened. "Your choice."

"I liked you better when you were dead," Charming said through gritted teeth. He stepped over to Daphne, who held out

Sabrina in her hands. "Personally, I think the girl looks better this way. Oh, very well. I suppose you kids will be registered voters eventually. Remember who did you a favor once."

Charming raised Sabrina's frog body to his face, closed his eyes, and planted a tiny peck on the top of her head. Sabrina felt the spell break immediately. There was a puff of smoke, and when it was clear she looked down, saw that her feet and hands were normal, and almost started dancing with happiness.

The mayor, on the other hand, looked as if he might barf and quickly wiped his mouth with a handkerchief.

Daphne raced to his side and wrapped him in a big hug. He struggled to free himself, but the little girl wouldn't let go. "I hope you win the election."

Charming smiled slightly and then managed to push her away. "Well, you don't have to worry. The latest polls say I'm going to win by a landslide. If all goes well, I think our friend the Queen of Hearts will soon be known as the Queen of Broken Hearts." He stepped over and pinned VOTE FOR CHARMING buttons on everyone's coats. When he got to Mr. Canis, he just set it in his hand.

"Remember, vote early and vote often. Now, if that's all you want, I'm a little busy at the moment. Not that this wasn't fun— but it wasn't. I trust you can find your way out," the mayor said, sticking his face in the old man's. "Don't forget to take your dog with you."

Canis snarled and closed his fist on the button. When he opened his hand, the pin was about the size of a dime. He dropped it on the floor at the mayor's feet.

Once they were outside and Charming had slammed the door, Sabrina turned to the old man.

"Are you going to tell Granny what I did?" Sabrina asked him.

Mr. Canis scowled and shook his head. "The disrespect you have for that woman is outrageous. Do you really think you're too clever for her? She knows every step you take. Relda Grimm is many things, but she is not stupid."

The old man darted into the woods behind Charming's house and disappeared.

10

THE FAMILY GATHERED AT THE DINING ROOM table with the three pieces of the sword.

"Maybe the witch tricked us," Sabrina said bitterly as she picked up the final piece and studied it closely. "Maybe this isn't the real blade."

She handed it to Uncle Jake, and he flipped it over, examining both sides. His face suddenly grew red, and he slammed the metal down on the table. "We've been on a wild goose chase!" he said. "We've been wasting our time all along!"

"It's not a fake. This is part of the Vorpal blade," Granny said. "Spaulding's description matches exactly."

"Well, a lot of good it's going to do us!" Uncle Jake shouted. He jumped up from his chair and stormed out of the room. A moment later they heard the front door slam. Sabrina went to follow, but Granny took her arm. "It's the magic, Sabrina. His coat pockets were filled with all kinds of things, and now they're gone. He's going to have a short temper until he gets over his cravings."

Sabrina understood perfectly. She was missing her wand and kept reaching into her pocket, only to find it wasn't there. She went to the closet, put on her coat, then pulled an old blanket off the top shelf.

"I'm going to keep him company," she said, then went outside.

Her uncle was pacing back and forth on the front porch. The sun was rising, but its rays had little effect on the sharp, cold air.

"Are you OK?" she asked.

"We were so close to fixing everything," Uncle Jake said. "Now we're back at a dead end, and there's nothing I can do about it. I hate feeling helpless."

Sabrina handed him the old blanket. Without his overcoat he was shivering. He wrapped it around his shoulders. "Thanks," he said.

"This is about more than just saving my mom and dad, isn't it?" Sabrina asked.

Uncle Jake nodded. "Mr. Canis was absolutely right. I was a problem child. I never listened to my parents. I snuck out. I got into all kinds of trouble. I was stubborn and thought I knew everything."

"You sound a lot like me," Sabrina admitted.

"But I was wrong, 'Brina," he said, taking her hands in his. "I should have listened. If I hadn't been so reckless, then maybe my dad wouldn't have died. It's my fault the Jabberwocky got loose and killed him. I made a stupid mistake twelve years ago, and it's still hurting this family. Hank and Veronica are suffering. You girls are suffering. My mother is suffering, and it's all my fault. Trying to save Hank and Veronica and kill the Jabberwocky were the only ways I knew to make things right. Maybe Mom would forgive me if I could fix things."

"She's your mother. She loves you."

Uncle Jake was quiet for a long time, then he stepped off the porch and started walking. "I just wanted to fix things," he said.

"Where are you going?" she asked, but he didn't answer, and soon he vanished down the road.

The girls finished their lunch of BLTs with something that tasted like bacon but had the texture of pudding. There were rose petal cookies for dessert. When their bellies were full, Granny collected the plates and took them into the kitchen. Daphne and Elvis ran upstairs to look after Puck. Sabrina went to the living room window and looked outside, hoping to spot Uncle Jake making his way up the driveway. He wasn't there.

"Your mustache and goatee are starting to fade," Granny said.

"I've been so busy I didn't even notice," Sabrina said, touching her lip lightly.

"Funny thing about time; it takes care of most problems," Granny said, as she sat on the sofa. She patted the cushion to her right, inviting Sabrina to join her. "If you wait long enough, even a mountain becomes a valley."

"OK, bring it on," Sabrina said, reluctantly taking a seat.

"What do you mean?"

"I know you're dying to give me a lecture on magic. I know you think it's better not to use it."

"You think I hate magic?" Granny said.

"You don't?"

"No. Magic can do amazing things. I just believe it should be used as a last resort," she said. "It shouldn't be the first answer to every problem, especially since it often leads to bigger troubles."

"Well, a little magic could come in handy every time I'm running away from something that's trying to eat me."

"You underestimate yourself, Sabrina. You don't need magic; you've got power coming out of your ears. You kept your sister safe for a year and a half in a very tough orphanage without magic. You escaped from one foster home after another without magic. You've been lost in the woods and chased by giants, you've foiled the destruction of this town, and you saved all of our lives a couple times over, and you did it all without magic. I know you think you're powerless, but you're wrong. You have a powerful heart, powerful friends, a powerful family, and a powerful mind. Giving magic to you, child, was a bit of overkill." The old woman looked at the clock. "Oh my, I'm late. Sabrina, do you think you could look after everyone for about half an hour?"

"You're leaving me here alone with Daphne?" Sabrina asked.

"Sure. You're eleven years old. I think you can be trusted for a little while," the old woman said. She took out a small whistle hanging from a chain around her neck and blew into it. Sabrina recognized it as the dog whistle the old woman used to call for Mr. Canis.

"You do?" Sabrina asked. "Why?"

"Because I *want* to trust you," Granny replied as she rushed to get her handbag. "I hate to leave, but we can't ignore one crisis while we're working on another. I have to go down to the school for the election. I'm afraid Mayor Charming is going to need every vote he can get."

She handed Sabrina the set of keys that unlocked everything in the house and in the Hall of Wonders. Sabrina looked down at them. It was an act of faith that no one had ever shown her before. A tear escaped her eye, but she quickly wiped it away.

"But what about my addiction to magic?" Sabrina asked.

"I've learned something from you, Sabrina. You can't run from your problems; you have to face them head-on. You'll never get over your need until you can walk away from it on your own."

"I'm nothing but a problem to you," Sabrina whispered.

The old woman hugged her. "If only everyone had the blessing of a problem like you."

The door opened, and Mr. Canis entered. "Have you found a way to mend the sword?"

"Not yet," Granny said, "but democracy is calling. Have you given any more thought to voting for Charming?"

Mr. Canis growled.

Granny laughed, and the two of them left. Seconds later, Sabrina heard the old family car's famous backfire, and then they were gone.

Sabrina tucked the key ring into her jeans and looked down at the broken pieces of the sword laid out on the table.

"Spaulding, what are you trying to tell us?"

Absentmindedly, she picked up the hilt of the Vorpal blade and aligned it with the broken pieces like she was working on a dangerously sharp jigsaw puzzle. When all the pieces were aligned, she stepped back and admired her work. It was a beautiful sword, if a weapon could be seen as art.

Suddenly, the inscriptions on each piece glowed green. The letters flashed bright red, then moved around of their own accord. A few of the letters vanished from the pieces of the blade they were on and reappeared on the piece that lacked an inscription. When this process was finished, it had a clue of its own glowing in a magical blue light.

LFEHAURBRA

"Spaulding! The final clue was waiting for us all along!" Sabrina cried. "But, who is L . . . fehaur . . . bra!"

"What's going on?" Daphne asked as she came down the stairs.

"Look!" Sabrina shouted. "The final clue!"

"I've never heard of anyone with that name," Daphne said, her face glowing in the light.

"And I've never come across it in the journals," Sabrina said.

"Maybe it's not a name. Maybe it's a word puzzle," Daphne said.

Sabrina grabbed her sister and gave her a hug. "Daphne, you're brilliant!"

"Of course I am," the little girl said.

"And we both know someone who likes word puzzles a lot," Sabrina said. "Come on!"

The two girls rushed up the steps, and Sabrina unlocked the door that led to Mirror's room.

"You stole Granny's keys," Daphne cried.

"No, she gave them to me. I'm babysitting you," Sabrina explained.

Daphne wrinkled up her nose. "That's crazy talk!"

Sabrina grabbed her sister's hand, and the two stepped inside the room. Sabrina braced for a lightning blast or a threatening ring of fire, but when Mirror's forbidding face appeared, two slices of cucumber covered his eyes.

"*Who dares enter my domain?*" he bellowed.

"Mirror! It's us!" Sabrina said.

Mirror reached up, removed a cucumber, and peered at the two girls with one squinty eye. The clouds behind him quickly disappeared.

"Howdy, Grimm sisters," Mirror said. "Sorry about all the theatrics. I'm in the middle of my skin-care regimen. These cucumbers are lifesavers for my bags, but it's a two-hour ordeal every morning. Do yourself a favor, girls, and don't get old."

"We've collected all the pieces of the Vorpal blade," Daphne said.

"Impressive," Mirror replied.

"Each of the pieces has a clue on it about how to find the next piece," Sabrina explained. "Unfortunately, the last piece had no hints until I lined the pieces together on the table. A new word appeared and lit up like fireworks."

"We don't understand it, but we thought you might," Daphne said.

Mirror looked surprised. "You want my help?"

"Well, I know you love word puzzles," Sabrina said.

Mirror grinned. "Wow! This is exciting. You know, most of the time I feel like I got stuck managing the supply closet while everyone else is out doing the fun stuff. I don't think anyone has ever asked for my help. Oh, I've been waiting for this for such a long time. Wait right here! This requires a costume change."

He vanished from the reflection, leaving the girls all alone.

"We're in a bit of a hurry," Sabrina called out to him.

A few moments later, he returned wearing an old-fashioned hat and chomping on a pipe. He looked like a supernatural Sherlock Holmes. "So, let's tackle this word of yours. What are the letters?"

"L-F-E-H-A-U-R-B-R-A," Sabrina said.

The letters suddenly appeared in the mirror's reflection. "What do you think it's supposed to tell you?" Mirror said.

"The Blue Fairy's secret identity," Daphne said.

Mirror's eyebrows rose in surprise. "Indeed! That is a big secret. Let's have a look."

Suddenly, the letters jumbled and were reformed into the words Brael Rufha.

"I've got it!" Mirror said proudly "The Blue Fairy is actually Brael Rufha!"

"Who?" the girls asked.

Mirror frowned. "OK. Let's try that again."

The letters jumbled and collected themselves into a new name: Harrab Fuel.

"I'm pretty sure there's no one in Ferryport Landing named Harrab Fuel," Sabrina said, trying to sound encouraging.

"I'm pretty sure no one in the world is named Harrab Fuel," Daphne added.

Mirror frowned at her, and the letters swirled a final time. They rearranged into the word "blue," leaving the F, H, A, R, R, and A on the other side alone.

"All right, Blue Fharra," Mirror said. "Anyone know someone named Blue Fharra?"

Sabrina jumped.

"You know, don't you?" Daphne asked.

"Could you move the H to the end?" Sabrina asked.

The letter floated over, making two new words: Blue Farrah.

"The waitress!" Daphne exclaimed. "Uncle Jake is not going to believe it. He's known her for years!"

"The Blue Fairy is a waitress?" Mirror asked.

"Yes," Sabrina said. "At the Blue-Plate Special. We met her yesterday."

"We've got to find her! But how? Granny and Mr. Canis are gone, and Uncle Jake ran away from home," Daphne said.

"He what?" Mirror asked.

"It's a long story," Sabrina said. "I have an idea."

She reached into her pocket and took out a business card—the same card Rip Van Winkle had handed her after his hair-raising drive to the school. Daphne spotted it, and a nervous smile slid onto her face.

"What about Puck? We can't leave him here alone," the little girl said.

"Mirror! Can you look after him?" Sabrina asked.

Mirror sighed. "Being a detective was fun while it lasted. Of course."

"C'mon," Sabrina said to her sister. "Help me move Mirror into Granny's room."

The girls reached down and lifted with all their might, awkwardly carrying the enormous mirror.

"Girls! Be careful!" Mirror cried. "If you break me, it's going to take more than some cucumbers on the eyes to fix the cracks."

When Rip Van Winkle's cab pulled into the driveway, the girls ran out and jumped into the backseat. Elvis tumbled in as well.

"Take us to the Blue-Plate Special," Sabrina cried.

A snort and then a low snore was the driver's response. Rip Van Winkle was already asleep.

"You've got to be kidding me!" Sabrina shouted.

"Wake up!" Daphne gave the man a good shake, but he didn't stir. Even when each girl grabbed an ear and shouted as loudly as they could into it, Mr. Van Winkle slumbered peacefully.

"Use the horn," Daphne said. "That's what woke him up the last time."

Sabrina leaped out of the car, opened the driver's door, and pushed down hard on the horn. There was a gassy wheeze followed by a clunk. Sabrina got down on her hands and knees. Underneath the car was a small, dangling mechanical device. She guessed it was the horn.

"It's broken!" she cried. "Everything on this car is broken. Even the driver!"

"What do we do? We have to get to the diner!"

Sabrina thought for a second, and a crazy idea leaped into her head. She'd seen people drive cars. All you had to do was steer, press the gas, or press the brake. How hard could it be? She remembered her father shouting at cabbies he was convinced were blind.

"Get up here in the front seat. I need your help," Sabrina said.

"You have a funny look on your face," Daphne said, as she did as she was told.

"We're driving."

"That's crazy talk!"

"Don't worry. I've been watching how it works."

Elvis let out a whine from the backseat.

"Daphne, we have to do this!" Sabrina continued.

The little girl threw her hands up in surrender, and together they pushed the old man to the passenger side of the cab.

"I need you to handle the pedals," Sabrina said. "My legs can't reach."

Daphne reluctantly crawled into the space beneath the dashboard.

"The one on the right is the gas and the other one is the brake," Sabrina explained.

"Again, crazy talk!" Daphne cried.

Sabrina climbed into the driver's seat, adjusted the mirrors, and closed the door. She pulled the seatbelt over her shoulder and locked it into place. Then she took a deep breath and turned the key. The car roared to life. She pulled the car's gearshift down into drive.

"OK, give it some gas," she said.

The wheels squealed, and the car lurched forward. "*Brake! Brake! Brake!*" she shouted, but they collided with the front porch. The mechanical Santa Claus sitting on the roof crashed down onto the hood of the car. Its robotic *Ho! Ho! Ho!* slowed and slurred until sparks shot out of Santa's ears and smoke billowed out from under his red cap.

"If I get coal for Christmas, I will never forgive you," Daphne said as she peeked over the dashboard at the mess.

"OK, relax," Sabrina said, doing her best to take her own advice. She looked down at the gearshift and guessed she needed to put the taxi into R if she wanted to back out of the driveway. She pulled on the stick, and the car rolled backward, veering into the yard but still finding its way to the street.

Daphne braked, and Sabrina put the car back into D for drive. The vehicle lurched forward, then puttered along at five miles an hour as Sabrina craned her neck to see over the dashboard.

"Give it some gas," Sabrina instructed.

"No!" Daphne said.

"C'mon! It will take us a week to get there at this rate."

Daphne scowled and pushed the gas pedal. The car leaped forward and tore off down the road. Sabrina did her best to keep the old taxi on the pavement, but it wasn't easy. The steering wheel had a significant pull to the right, and the car kept careening into people's yards.

"There's a red light coming," Sabrina said.

Daphne pushed hard on the brake, and the car screeched to a stop, causing Elvis to roll off the backseat and onto the floor.

The sudden starts and stops went on for several miles, with the girls passing only a few curious drivers who wisely steered their cars far away from the jalopy. It looked to Sabrina as if they were going to make it to the diner without too much damage, until they made a turn into Ferryport Landing's business district. She had always thought of the town as a slow, dull place. Now it looked like an obstacle course of possible disasters. There was not a lot of traffic, but parked cars lined both sides of the road. She urged Daphne to slow the car down, but Sabrina still slammed into several of them. Car alarms blasted, startling her and causing her to jerk the cab to the other side of the road where she found herself in the oncoming traffic lane. She scraped against the cars to her left, leaving sparks and scratched paint for blocks.

Finally, they arrived at the Blue-Plate Special and pulled into the parking lot. The girls hopped out, leaving Mr. Van Winkle sleeping soundly, and along with Elvis they sprinted through the front door. The little bell rang loudly, causing a few customers to look up from their coffees and newspapers to see what all the commotion was about.

A heavyset waitress with tight brown curls and old-lady spectacles appeared with a handful of menus. When she saw Elvis, she frowned. "Oh, girls, I'm sorry. We can't let you bring your . . . is that a dog?"

Sabrina ignored the question. "I'm looking for Farrah," she said, as she and her sister scanned the restaurant. A horrible feeling crept over her as she eyed the diner. Just two days ago this place had been a war zone. The Jabberwocky and Red Riding Hood had carved a path of destruction that only magic could have fixed in such a short time. Glinda the Good Witch and the rest of the Three often took care of such work for the mayor. It was their job to sprinkle forgetful dust on any non-Everafters traumatized by the unexpected appearance of monsters and the unexplained. *What if Farrah had taken advantage of the opportunity and made sure she was forgotten as well?*

"Honey, she's not here," the waitress said.

Sabrina felt relief. "Do you know where she is?"

"Why, she's on her lunch break," the waitress said with a bit of irritation.

Just then there was a loud thump that knocked a coffeepot to the floor. It shattered, sending coffee and glass everywhere.

"Uh-oh," Daphne said, flashing her sister a worried look.

Sabrina grabbed the waitress by the shoulders. "Do you know where Farrah went?"

"Probably down to the elementary school. Today is election day," the woman snapped.

"We have to go to the school," Sabrina cried, and she, Daphne, and Elvis made a mad dash back to the cab as a second loud thump lifted the taxi right off the ground.

"Uh, we have a little problem," Daphne said, as they crawled back into their seats.

The girls stared into the rearview mirror. Standing behind the car were Red Riding Hood and her hulking nightmare, which panted eagerly as if awaiting permission to rip them all limb from limb.

11

SABRINA NEARLY BROKE OFF THE GEARSHIFT
when she slammed it into drive. Daphne pressed hard
on the gas until the pedal was on the car's floorboard.
The engine roared, and the car lunged forward and raced across
the parking lot; unfortunately, it didn't get far. The Jabberwocky
leaped into the air and landed in their path.

"*Brakes!*" Sabrina shouted, and Daphne obliged. The car slid to
a stop inches from the monster's scaly leg.

Red Riding Hood skipped over to the car and tried to open the
door, but Sabrina reached over just in time to lock it. The little girl
scowled and pointed to the door. Her pet stepped over and tore it
off its hinges.

"I know you are trying to ruin my game," Red Riding Hood
said. "But I won't let you."

Sabrina slammed the car into reverse and steered it into the street. Then she put it in drive and made a hard right at the next intersection. Unfortunately, when she checked her rearview mirror, the Jabberwocky was still behind them, with Red Riding Hood on its shoulders.

Sabrina made a left and then a quick right. But no matter how fast the cab went or how many turns she made, the monster and its mistress were gaining ground. They raced along the road that lined the Hudson River until Sabrina saw the school. Red, white, and blue banners were everywhere, encouraging people to vote for mayor of Ferryport Landing. A small crowd of people stood outside in the parking lot, and a few others shuffled out of the school's wide-open main doors.

"There it is! Brake!" Sabrina said, as she made a rough turn, hit a patch of ice, and sailed across the parking lot like a runaway train. "Brake again!"

Daphne did as she was told, but the old cab's bald tires had no traction, and the vehicle slid right through the main doors and down the main hallway of the school. Voters screamed and leaped out of the way, narrowly escaping as the big car careened past them. The old jalopy crashed through the gymnasium's double doors and came to a stop.

A crowd gathered around as the girls climbed out. Many of them were outraged and demanding answers. Sabrina tried to warn them about the monsters chasing them, but no one would listen. Granny and Mr. Canis pushed through the mob and stood between it and the girls. The throngs of people quickly grew quiet. Sabrina wondered why, then noticed Mr. Canis staring everyone down. He sniffed the air wildly, then raised an alarmed eyebrow.

"Relda, the monster is coming. We have to get the humans to safety," he growled.

"A monster?" one woman cried. "Is he serious?"

"He's right," Sabrina said. "We don't have time to explain, but he's not kidding. A real live monster is headed this way."

"Relda, what is going on here?" Charming demanded.

"Later, Billy," Sabrina snapped. "We need to get these people out of here. There's a Jabberwocky coming."

"Mr. Seven! Pull that fire alarm!" the mayor commanded. Mr. Seven rushed to the alarm and yanked it down hard. A siren wailed, drawing everyone's attention.

"There is a fire in the boiler room, people," Charming shouted. "Please evacuate to the parking lot."

"Thanks, Mayor," Granny Relda said. "Now, girls, tell us what is going on."

"We know who the Blue Fairy is," Daphne said. She reached into the car and snatched the bag that contained the broken sword and handed it to her grandmother. "She's a waitress at the Blue Plate Special. Her name is Farrah."

"Who in the blazes is Farrah?" the mayor cried.

From the evacuating crowd stepped the waitress. She still had on her work uniform with its little nametag. She looked bewildered and vulnerable. "I am."

"I'm sorry to do this to you," Granny said, handing her the sack. "I know how important your privacy is, but we are in the middle of a dire emergency."

"Of course," Farrah said, then looked at the pieces of the magical sword. She removed the bubble gum from her mouth, stuffed it into a wad of paper, and closed her eyes. Suddenly, a sky-blue light began to seep out of her clothing. It engulfed her body and grew so bright that it made her impossible to look at. When the light dimmed, Farrah the waitress was gone. In her place was a tall, beautiful woman with light blue hair and skin like milk. Her eyes were twinkling stars, and she had two pink-streaked wings on her back that fluttered softly.

"It's the Blue Fairy," someone said from the crowd. Many of the Everafters crowded around to get a good look at the legendary figure.

The Blue Fairy held out her hand, and a little ball of blue light appeared. It crackled with electricity. The ball zipped out of her hand and flew into the sack that held the sword pieces, filling it with magical light. After a moment, the light dimmed, and the Blue Fairy reached inside. When she removed her hand, she was holding the Vorpal blade, perfect and whole.

Granny took it eagerly from the woman and thanked her.

"Relda, give me the sword," Mr. Canis said. "You can't handle the monster and the child."

"You are in no condition, old friend. Don't worry; I've had to fight a lot of monsters in my day. I suspect there will be plenty more," she said, then turned to the crowd. "Folks, I recommend that you find somewhere safe to hide. Something wicked this way comes."

As if on cue, the Jabberwocky, with Red Riding Hood on its shoulders, stepped into the room. The monster set the little girl on the ground and sized up the crowd as if deciding whom to eat and in what order.

"Grandma! Doggy!" Red Riding Hood cried, as she rushed toward Granny Relda and Mr. Canis. "I have my family back. Now we can play house."

Granny lifted the sword threateningly.

"My, what a big sword you have, Grandma," Red Riding Hood continued.

"Child, I am not your grandmother," Granny said. "The two people you have kidnapped are not your mother and father. Your family is dead. They died hundreds of years ago. Pretending to have a family is not the same as having one."

"But we can play house," the little girl said.

"Playtime is over, little one. Where are Henry and Veronica Grimm?"

Sabrina thought she saw a glimmer of understanding in the little girl's face.

As she stared up at Granny Relda, Red Riding Hood seemed to have a million terrible questions to ask. Maybe it was all too overwhelming for her, because she shook her head violently, and her face contorted back into its insane expression.

"Kitty! Let's take Grandma and doggy home with us," she shouted.

Granny raised the Vorpal blade to defend herself, but the monster was on top of her in a flash. It grabbed her around the waist and lifted her off the ground. The old woman dropped the sword, and it clanged loudly on the gymnasium floor.

"Granny!" the girls shouted.

Mr. Canis leaped at the beast, but a flick of its tail sent the old man sailing across the room and into the crowd.

"I'll go for the sword," Sabrina told her sister. She dashed across the floor, but before she could reach it, the monster slammed its foot down on top of it. Sabrina tried to pull it out from under the beast, but she wasn't strong enough.

Just then, Sheriff Hamstead rushed through the crowd. He had his billy club held high. "Put her down!" he shouted. The monster turned toward the pudgy policeman and swatted the cop across the gym with one of its fearsome paws. Hamstead landed painfully at the foot of the podium. Snow White tried to rush to his side, but Charming grabbed her arm and held her back.

"I have to help them," Snow White cried.

"You'll get yourself killed," he said. "There's nothing anyone in this room can do to stop that thing."

"Billy, what happened to you?" Snow White asked. "When did you get so cowardly?"

Sabrina tugged at the sword once more, but she still couldn't free it. When the monster turned all of its attention on her, Daphne took advantage of its distraction. Sabrina watched helplessly as her sister rushed to the monster's side.

"First you bow to your opponent," Daphne said, then bowed to the monster that was now hovering over her.

"Daphne, no!" Sabrina cried.

"Don't worry. Ms. White taught my class that these moves will stop an attacker much bigger than me." She turned back to the beast. "Move into an offensive stance."

Daphne shifted her body into her attack position with fists clenched.

"Present your warrior face! Argggghhhh!"

The beast looked down at her and roared so loudly that Daphne's hair flew back. Unfazed by the monster's scream, the little girl rushed forward.

"Deliver attack!" She kicked the Jabberwocky in the leg, but her assault was like a mosquito biting an elephant. The beast reached down and picked Daphne up off the floor with its free hand. Now it had both Sabrina's grandmother and her sister in its deadly claws.

Sabrina searched the crowd of Everafters for help. Ms. White looked as if she wanted to, but she was held fast by Charming. Mr. Canis and Sheriff Hamstead were still recovering from the Jabberwocky's attack. The Queen of Hearts stood off to the side with a wicked smile. Most everyone else was cowering in fear. There were no heroes to save them.

Suddenly, Mayor Charming leaped onto the Jabberwocky's back. He wrapped his arms around its neck and pummeled it in the ear. Moments later, Charming was flung to the floor, but his sudden attack had surprised the creature, and it dropped Granny Relda and Daphne.

The monster roared in frustration and took a step toward the family. It was all Sabrina needed. She snatched the blade off the ground and held it over her head. One swift slice would bring her family home. It would get Puck to safety. Suddenly, there was a *pop!* She turned and saw Uncle Jake.

"Sorry to keep you waiting, ladies," Uncle Jake said, helping his mother and Daphne to their feet. He tapped the Nome King's belt wrapped around his waist and shrugged. "Do you know how hard it is to find thirty size D batteries?"

"The Jabberwocky's impossible to stop," Sabrina said.

"'Brina, this belongs to me," Jake said, as he took the sword away from her.

Sabrina looked into his face and saw a broken heart finally getting its revenge. This monster had killed Uncle Jake's father. It had decimated his family, forcing his mother to erase his existence. It had helped kidnap his brother and sister-in-law. It had brought tragedy to three generations of Grimms. She stepped aside, letting Uncle Jake walk calmly over to the Jabberwocky. He was as tall and confident as if he had been preparing for this moment his whole life. He glanced over at Red Riding Hood as if to say, *It's over*, and then plunged the sword into the beast's chest, right where the monster's heart might have been. The blade sank deep into its flesh.

The Jabberwocky's death cry was oddly faint and pathetic. There was a moment of calm on the beast's face, and then it fell over as if it had been pushed. The crash caused the gymnasium's shiny new hardwood floor to buckle. The monster's little leathery wings flapped for a few moments, then grew still.

"You killed the kitty!" Red Riding Hood raged. "You ruined the game!"

Daphne stepped over to the girl, bowed, presented her warrior face, and then punched Red Riding Hood in the face. Red Riding Hood fell over unconscious.

"Crazy talk," Daphne said to the crumpled girl.

Uncle Jake yanked the blade from the monster and held it in his hands. He looked as if he wanted to kill it all over again.

"It's over, Jake," Granny said.

"Is it?" he asked, as several Everafters approached: Snow White, Sheriff Hamstead, the Queen of Hearts, Sheriff Nottingham, and a collection of talking animals, Munchkins, and trolls. The Blue Fairy was at their center.

"This is an outrage!" the Queen of Hearts screamed. "This was a deliberate act by Mayor Charming and his cronies, the Grimm family, to disrupt this election. I wouldn't be surprised if this was an attempt to sway voters into believing the family has value in this community. Well, it won't work!"

"If you don't shut your mouth right now, I'm going to shut it for you," Snow White said.

"You insolent cow," Nottingham said. "You may be the mayor's trollop, but your demands mean little to me." He pulled his sword from his waist and stalked toward the Grimms. "Even if we don't win this election, things are going to change right now."

Suddenly, an arrow zipped through the air and impaled Nottingham's hand. His sword fell to the ground, and he cried out in agony.

"You won't lay a hand on the Grimms as long as I live," a voice bellowed. Sabrina turned and nearly fell over in shock. Mayor

Charming stood on the stage, with a bow in his hand and another arrow set to fly. A man in a green suit stood next to him. He had bright red hair and a bushy goatee.

"Is that Robin Hood?" Daphne cried. She was biting her palm before her grandmother could confirm his identity.

"I told you Charming was in league with the Grimms," the queen cried.

"Think what you want," Charming said. "But they're going home today, safe and sound. Right after they vote for me, of course. And, Nottingham—the next time you call the woman I love a trollop, you'll find an arrow in your throat."

Nottingham scowled and stormed out of the room. Charming handed the bow and arrow back to his friend. "Thank you, Robin," he said.

"He saved us," Sabrina said, somewhat bewildered.

"Ending his career in politics in the process, I fear," Granny Relda replied. "Look at the crowd. He just lost this election."

"Why would he do that?" Daphne asked.

Granny pointed at the mayor. He and Snow White were kissing passionately, as if they were the only two people on the planet.

"Love can make a hero out of anyone," Granny replied.

"I knew he was one of the good guys," Daphne said.

"Good people of Ferryport Landing, don't let these cheap distractions stop you from casting your ballots," the queen said. "This is exactly the kind of nonsense that needs to change."

"You want change?" Uncle Jake shouted. "I'll give you change!" He spun around, grabbed the Blue Fairy around the neck, and held the Vorpal blade to her throat.

"Jake, what are you doing?" Granny cried.

"There's more to fix!" Uncle Jake shouted. "And the Blue Fairy is going to help me."

"What do you want?" the Blue Fairy asked softly.

"Is it true that if I wish for something you have to fulfill it?"

The radiant fairy nodded.

"Then I want a wish," Uncle Jake said.

"Uncle Jake!" Sabrina cried. "What are you thinking? She helped us."

"Say your wish, Jacob Grimm," the fairy said.

"I wish I had all of your power!" Uncle Jake said.

The Blue Fairy smiled and nodded as if what he was asking for was simple. A swirl of light and mist encircled her, then turned into a pulsating orb as big as a baseball. It flew at Uncle Jake, hitting him hard in the chest with a tremendous explosion that knocked everyone off their feet. When Sabrina stood up again, she saw Farrah the waitress lying on the floor nearby. Her magic was gone.

"Hey, 'Brina," Uncle Jake said behind her. She spun around to face him. Two pink-streaked wings suddenly popped out of his back, and he turned his head to admire them. They flapped and lifted him off the ground, allowing him to hover above the crowd. He laughed like a child on Christmas morning. "You wouldn't believe the power. I can do almost anything I want. Anything!"

Granny Relda was full of despair. "Jake, what have you done?"

"It's not what I've done, Mom," he said as he floated back down to the ground and kissed her on the cheek. "It's what I'm going to do. And to make it happen, I'm going to need even more magic!"

He looked out over the crowd of Everafters and his face grew serious. His hands rose in the air, and a bright blue ball appeared in them. It shot electrical charges through the crowd, hitting every Everafter squarely in the chest. Mr. Canis fell to his knees. Snow White collapsed on Charming, who fell himself. The White Rabbit tumbled to the ground and was squished by Beauty and her beastly husband. Ogres, cyclopes, trolls, witches, and even fairy godmothers fell to the floor.

"What are you doing to them?" Sabrina asked.

"I'm taking the magic that makes them immortal. I need it!" he shouted as the energy surged through him. His eyes disappeared and were replaced with a fiery light. Cracks appeared all over his body as if it were just a useless shell, and then a light flashed through the gymnasium that was so bright Sabrina had to close her eyes. Uncle Jake rocketed off the ground, through the roof, and into the sky. Rubble and debris fell from the ceiling. Sabrina grabbed her grandmother and sister and pulled them to safety.

"What's he doing?" Daphne asked, but Granny didn't answer. She stared at the hole in the roof. Sabrina had her eyes elsewhere. The Everafters scattered around the gym were growing older at an alarming rate. Prince Charming's youthful, handsome face began to sag. His eyes took on a slightly yellow tint, and his hair started falling out. He was becoming an old man right before her eyes. He reached out for her with a bony, frail hand.

Mr. Canis morphed into the Wolf, but the beast wasn't intimidating or deadly. He struggled with age as his dark brown coat turned white and his eyes grew cloudy with blindness.

"Look!" Daphne said as she pointed to the ceiling. Uncle Jake was back.

He descended like an angel enveloped in a light so bright the girls had to look away. When he landed on the ground, he smiled at his family, and the light faded. The Uncle Jake that Sabrina knew was gone, replaced with someone completely new who seemed to be made of diamonds. The only familiar thing left, she noticed, was his quirky, mischievous grin. He stepped forward to hug the two sisters, but they stepped back in fear.

"What have you done?" Sabrina asked.

"I'm granting myself a wish," he replied. "I wanted to be

powerful enough to make the people I love happy. I've been miserable, Sabrina. Happy is better. You can be happy, too. Wish for something. Anything. I can make it happen."

"But look at the cost!" Granny Relda said as she hovered over Mayor Charming's elderly body. Snow White lay next to him, reaching for his hand with her bony, arthritic fingers. "The price is too high."

"Don't cry for them," Uncle Jake said. "The Everafters have had their day in the sun, and it was a long, long day. With their power, I can re-create this world as a paradise where 'happily ever after' isn't just for a bunch of bedtime stories come to life. It's time for all of our dreams to come true! And I'm starting with you."

Suddenly, the pulsating blue orb reappeared in his hand. It twisted and turned until it divided itself in two, creating an identical twin. He tossed the second orb to the ground at Granny Relda's feet, and once it was at rest it grew in size, morphing and bending. When the transformation was complete, an old man stood in its place. He had broad shoulders, blond-streaked gray hair, a beard, and a familiar toothy smile. Sabrina had seen him many times in photographs hanging throughout the house, but that was the only place the old man still existed. He was Basil Grimm, the girls' grandfather and Granny Relda's husband.

"Relda?" the old man asked, looking slightly confused.

Granny Relda burst into tears and buried her face in her hands.

The old man rushed to her side and embraced her, but she pulled away.

"It's not right," the old woman said. "Send him back."

"No!" Uncle Jake cried. Discouraged, he turned to Daphne and smiled. "I know something you want." The blue orb divided again, and the man tossed its duplicate at the little girl's feet. Once again, the orb grew and morphed—but this time, instead of creating another person, it became a door, standing in space, and someone was knocking on the other side.

"Open it," the man said. "It's for you."

Daphne backed away from the door and shook her head. Uncle Jake seemed disappointed, but he raised his hand and the door swung open on its own. Behind the door were Henry and Veronica Grimm. They rushed through the doorway and swept the little girl up in their arms, kissing her over and over dozens of times. Henry and Veronica raced to Sabrina and embraced her as well.

"It's like a dream," Sabrina said.

"OK, 'Brina, what'll it be?" Uncle Jake said. "Make a wish. But I already know what you want. You want power, and not like that crummy wand you had to surrender. I'm talking real power—the kind that moves mountains and boils rivers. Your family would never die. You would always be happy. No more monsters. No more fairy tales. You could change everything."

Sabrina's heart raced with possibilities. Just standing near

Uncle Jake was an incredible feeling, more intense than holding Merlin's wand, more like *being* the wand itself. With the kind of power Uncle Jake offered, she could erase the last year and a half like it had never happened: no orphanage, no giants, no monsters, no bad guys. She could heal Puck. There were no limits to the possibilities. Her imagination washed over her, showing her millions of options for a happy life.

"Sabrina," Granny said, "how much are you willing to pay?"

Sabrina glanced around the room at the Everafters. Some of them were pulling in their final breaths. Was her happiness worth their lives?

"I know what I want, Uncle Jake," Sabrina said.

Uncle Jake smiled and gave her a wink. "Make it count!"

"Uncle Jake, you're smart, you've got a great family, and you're a Grimm," Sabrina said. "I wish that deep down you had always known how much power that gave you."

Uncle Jake looked strange. His eyes welled with tears, and the world started to rumble. A flood of memories rolled through Sabrina's mind, new memories that had never existed before. She saw how she'd met her Uncle Jake and how he'd taught her to use the wand. She watched Granny Relda catch them in the Hall of Wonders, and their battle with the Jabberwocky at the diner. She even saw the dramatic return of Mr. Canis. It all happened the same way, except for one shocking difference. When Uncle Jake killed the Jabberwocky, the fight was over. He didn't attack the Blue Fairy. He never stole the life force out of the Everafters. He was content with how the battle ended, and he hugged his mother.

Sabrina opened her eyes. Her grandfather was gone and so were her parents. The Everafters were alive and well and gathered around her. The Queen of Hearts was still filling the air with her angry tirade, and the Jabberwocky was still dead at their feet. The Blue Fairy stood next to her, smiling. "Thank you, Sabrina," she said, and then she transformed into a glowing orb and zipped away, out the double doors, and out of sight.

Uncle Jake stepped over to Red Riding Hood, snatched the magical ring off the unconscious girl's finger, and tucked it into his pants pocket. Granny frowned, but Uncle Jake just laughed. "Don't worry, Mom. It's going straight into the Hall of Wonders for safekeeping."

"Hello, Grandma," Red Riding Hood said, waking up and climbing to her feet. "My kitty is dead."

"Child, I am not your—"

"Play along," Sabrina suggested.

Granny looked unsure, but nodded. "We don't need the kitty to play games. We can play without him."

Red Riding Hood looked to the ceiling as if debating what the old woman was saying. A smile crossed her face, and she clapped her hands. "Okeydokey!"

"But before we play games, we need our whole family together, right?"

The little girl nodded.

"So we need to find the mommy and the daddy and the baby brother, and then we'll all go and get the puppy, and then we can play house. Does that sound fun?"

"Yes, I want to play house," the child repeated. "But the Master will be mad if I tell."

"The Master?" Sabrina asked.

"Yes, he will be very mad. He wants to keep the mommy and the daddy and the baby brother. He wants me to paint the red hands everywhere I go. I try to be good. The Master can get angry."

"She's not the leader of the Scarlet Hand," Daphne said to her sister.

"Well, I don't think the Master would mind if we all played, would he?" Granny asked.

"I guess not," the little girl said.

Once Red revealed their whereabouts, Sheriff Hamstead had Henry and Veronica's sleeping bodies transported to Granny's house in an ambulance. Now they would rest on a queen-sized bed inside the room that also housed the magic mirror.

"Are they sick?" Daphne asked as she held her mother's hand.

"No, *liebling*. Just sleeping," Granny Relda said.

Sabrina put her head on her father's chest and heard his heart beating. Then she sat up and kissed him on the forehead. "Did they find the baby?" she asked.

"No sign of him," Sheriff Hamstead said. "Just an empty bassinet."

"Who do you think he belongs to?" Daphne wondered.

"It's hard to say, but I feel terrible for his parents. They must be so distraught," Granny said.

"Why won't Mom and Dad wake up?" Sabrina asked.

"It's a sleeping spell," Granny explained.

"And a strong one at that," Mirror said as his face appeared in the reflection. "We don't have anything in the Hall of Wonders that can break it."

"Then what can we do?" Sabrina asked.

"These sleeping spells . . . some of them are fairly normal potions, sometimes poisoned flowers or apples, but overwhelmingly they are cast by someone with a vendetta against the victim," Uncle Jake said. "Luckily, even bad magic has a backup plan, and in nearly every case I've ever heard, the spell can be broken with a kiss."

Elvis hopped up on his back paws and licked Veronica on the face.

"Sorry, Elvis. It has to be a romantic kiss from someone who truly loves them," Granny Relda explained.

"If one of them was awake, then this would be no problem," Mr. Canis said.

"Wait, if that's how you break the spell, how are we going to wake them?" Sabrina asked. "My parents love each other. They're the only ones who could wake each other up."

When no one answered, Sabrina thought she might cry.

"We'll find a way," Granny said, as she took Sabrina into her arms.

"In the meantime, we should address the problem with Puck," Mr. Canis said. "He is growing weaker. If we can use the Vorpal blade to cut a big enough hole in the barrier, I'd like to take the car and get the boy to his people."

"I'll go with you," Hamstead said. "I happen to be between jobs at the moment."

"The Queen of Hearts won the election?" Daphne asked.

"By a landslide," Hamstead grumbled.

"Oh, dear," Granny said.

Sabrina stared down at her parents. She knew they would understand. "I'll go, too. Puck would never have been hurt if he weren't trying to help us find Mom and Dad. I owe it to him."

"Me, too!" Daphne said.

"Jacob, can I trust you in the house all alone?" Granny asked her son.

Uncle Jake smiled. "Probably not, but I'll keep the place safe."

❧

Mr. Canis helped Granny Relda place Puck in the front seat of the car, then helped her into her seat. When everyone was squeezed into the jalopy, Uncle Jake waved and wished them all the luck in the world.

"You be careful among the fairy folk," Uncle Jake said. "If you think this town is full of nuts, you haven't seen anything yet."

"We'll be careful," Sabrina said.

"Take care of my Elvis," Daphne said. The big dog leaped up to her window and gave her a farewell lick on the face.

Mr. Canis started the car and backed it out of the driveway.

"We're an odd group of people for an adventure, don't you think?" Hamstead squealed.

Granny smiled. "Pig and Wolf and Grandma. Who would have thought it?"

Even Mr. Canis laughed. Sabrina hoped he would never do it again. It was an obnoxious, snorty sound.

Daphne hugged her sister. "This isn't exactly how I pictured our first Christmas in Ferryport Landing."

Sabrina gazed out the window as the car rolled down the road. Would they be able to save Puck? Would they find a way to wake their parents? And would the Grimm family ever get its happily ever after?

ENJOY THIS
SNEAK PEEK FROM

4

THE SISTERS GRIMM

~ ONCE UPON A CRIME ~

1

THE EXPLOSION SHOOK SABRINA GRIMM SO
hard she swore she felt her brain do a somersault inside her skull. As she struggled to get her bearings, a
noxious black smoke choked her and burned her eyes. Could she
escape? No, she was at the mercy of a cold, soulless machine: the
family car.

"Isn't anyone worried that this hunk of junk might kill us?"
Sabrina yelled, but no one heard her over the chaos. As usual,
she was the only person in her family who noticed anything was
wrong. Murder plots; horrifying monsters; the shaking, jostling,
rattling death trap the family used to get around: Sabrina had her
eyes wide open to trouble. She was sure if she didn't stay on her
toes her entire family would be dead by nightfall on any given day.
They were lucky to have her.

Her grandmother, a kind, sweet lady, was in the front seat, buried in the same book she had been reading for the last two hours. Next to her was the old woman's constant companion: a skinny, grouchy old man named Mr. Canis, who drove the family everywhere. Sharing the backseat with Sabrina was a portly, pink-skinned fellow named Ernest Hamstead, and nestled between them was Daphne, Sabrina's seven-year-old sister, who slumbered peacefully, drooling like a faucet onto Sabrina's coat sleeve. Sabrina gently nudged her sister toward Mr. Hamstead. He grimaced when he noticed the drool and shot Sabrina a look that said, "Thanks for nothing."

Sabrina pretended not to notice and leaned forward to get her grandmother's attention. Granny Relda set her book down in her lap and turned to Sabrina with a smile. The old woman's face was lined in wrinkles, but her pink cheeks and button nose gave her a youthful appearance. She always wore colorful dresses and matching hats with a sunflower appliqué in the center. Today she was in purple.

"Where are we?" Sabrina shouted.

Her grandmother cupped a hand to her ear to let Sabrina know she hadn't heard the question over the car's terrific racket.

"Are we getting close to the fairy kingdom yet?"

"Oh, I love chili, but I'm afraid it doesn't love me," Granny shouted back.

"No, not chili! The fairy kingdom!" Sabrina cried. "Are we getting close?"

"Why no, I've never kissed a monkey. What an odd question."

Sabrina was about to throw up her hands in defeat when Mr. Canis turned to her. "We are not far," he barked, then turned his gaze back to the road. The old man had better hearing than anyone.

Sabrina sighed with relief. All the rumbling and sputtering would soon be over, and it would all have been worth it to help save Puck. The shivering boy was huddled next to her grandmother, his blond hair matted down and his face drenched in sweat. Sabrina felt a pang of regret. If it weren't for her, he wouldn't have been at death's door at all.

She sat back in her seat just as the car came to a stop at an intersection. She looked out the window. To the left was farmland as far as she could see, to the right a dusty country road leading to a tiny, distant farmhouse. Behind her was her new hometown, Ferryport Landing, and ahead . . . she wasn't sure. A place where Puck could get some help for his injuries, a place her grandmother said was filled with people like him—fairies.

As the car rolled forward, Sabrina lost herself in memories. She'd once been a normal kid living on the Upper East Side of Manhattan, with a mom and a dad, a little sister, and an apartment near Carl Schurz Park. Life was simple and easy and ordinary. Then one day her parents, Henry and Veronica, vanished. The police searched for them, but all they found was their abandoned car and a single clue—a red handprint left in paint on the dashboard.

No one came forward to take care of the girls, so Sabrina and Daphne were placed in an orphanage and assigned to Minerva Smirt, an ill-tempered caseworker who hated children. She took a special dislike to the Grimm sisters and for almost a year and a half she dumped them with foster families who used and abused them. These so-called loving caregivers forced the girls to be their personal maids, pool cleaners, and—once—ditch diggers. More often than not, the families were in it for the state check, but some were just plain crazy.

When Granny Relda finally found the sisters and took them in, Sabrina was sure the old woman was a nutcase, like all the rest. Their father had told them that his mother had died before they were born, so this grandmother had to be an imposter. When the old woman moved the girls to a little town on the Hudson River called Ferryport Landing, miles from civilization, she claimed her neighbors were all fairy-tale characters. She told the girls the mayor was Prince Charming, the Three Little Pigs ran the police department, witches served pancakes at the diner, and ogres delivered the mail. She also claimed that Sabrina and Daphne were the last living descendants of Jacob and Wilhelm, the Brothers Grimm, whose book of fairy tales wasn't fiction but an account of actual events and the beginning of extensive recordkeeping by each new generation. Granny said it was the Grimm legacy to investigate any unusual crimes and to keep an eye on the mischief-making fairy-tale folk, also known as Everafters. In a nutshell, the girls were the next in a long line of "fairy-tale detectives."

Sabrina had been sure this "grandmother" had forgotten to take her medication—that is, until a giant came along and kidnapped the old woman. Suddenly, her stories held a lot more weight. After the sisters Grimm rescued her, they agreed to become fairy-tale detectives—Daphne enthusiastically, Sabrina reluctantly—and plunged headfirst into investigating the other freaky felonies of their new hometown.

Daphne loved every minute of their new lives. What seven-year-old wouldn't want to live next door to her favorite bed-time stories? But Sabrina couldn't adjust to the strange characters they encountered. She distrusted the Everafters, and it was no secret that many in the community felt the same way about her family. Most thought the Grimms were meddlers. Others downright despised them. Sabrina really couldn't blame them. After all, the Everafters were trapped in Ferryport Landing because of a two-hundred-year-old magical spell cast by her great-great-great-great-grandfather, Wilhelm Grimm. Ever since, a magical barrier surrounded the town in an invisible bubble that no Everafter could pierce. Wilhelm had been trying to prevent a war, but all the Everafters, whether good or bad, were trapped. Many of them looked at the Grimms as if they were prison guards.

But the real reason Sabrina didn't trust the Everafters was that red handprint. It was the mark of a secret organization called the Scarlet Hand, and it was popping up all over town. No one knew the identity of its members, or that of the mysterious leader they followed, a shadowy figure known only as the Master.

There was some good news: Henry and Veronica were physically recovered from their kidnappers and at that moment were safe in Granny's home. But, unfortunately, they were under a magic spell of their own—one that kept them from waking up. Uncle Jake was with them now, working hard to find a way to interrupt their seemingly eternal sleep.

Puck had been injured helping to rescue them. He and the Grimm sisters fought the demented Red Riding Hood and her ferocious pet, the Jabberwocky. The monster had ripped Puck's fairy wings off of his back, and now he was dangerously ill. Lucky for everyone, the Grimm family had in its possession a magical sword called the Vorpal blade that they used to kill the Jabberwocky. Rumor had it the steel's sharp edge could cut through anything, including the magical barrier. The rumors proved to be true. Mr. Canis used it to cut a hole big enough for the family car to drive through, then he hid the sword in a place where Uncle Jake could find it later in order to store it safely.

Out of the corner of her eye, Sabrina spotted blue-and-red lights flashing behind them.

"What's going on?" Sabrina asked.

"The police are asking us to pull over," Mr. Hamstead said. He and Mr. Canis shared a concerned look, as the old man steered to the side of the road. Canis himself was not well. Lately, he'd been experiencing a change in his appearance that got more and more obvious by the day. Sabrina quietly prayed the officer wouldn't notice.

There was a tap on Mr. Canis's window, and a very angry police officer, wearing a short navy blue coat and sunglasses, peeked inside. He eyed the family suspiciously.

"Do you know why I pulled you over?" he asked.

"Were we speeding?" Mr. Canis asked.

"Speeding? No, I pulled you over because this . . . this tank you're driving is violating at least a hundred different environmental and safety laws. Let me see your driver's license."

Mr. Canis shared a troubled glance with Granny Relda, then turned back to face the policeman. "I'm afraid I don't have one."

Sabrina cringed. This was news to her.

The policeman laughed in disbelief. "You've got to be kidding me. OK, folks, everyone out of the car."

"Officer, I'm sure we can—"

The officer bent down. "Step out of the car," he said sternly.

"OK, let's get out of the car," Hamstead said calmly.

Daphne was still sound asleep, so Sabrina shook the little girl until she opened her eyes.

"Whazzabigidea?" Daphne grumbled.

"Get up, we're going to jail," Sabrina said, helping her out of the car.

They were stopped on a bridge, and the wind coming off the water below was brutal. Cars and trucks whizzed by, kicking up even more wind. The cold air chilled Sabrina to the bone. It was a terrible day, and the dark clouds hanging in the sky warned that it was only going to get worse.

"Officer, if I could be of any assistance," Mr. Hamstead said as he tugged his pants up over his belly, "I happen to be the former sheriff of Ferryport Landing, and—"

"Where?"

"Ferryport Landing. It's about two hours north."

"Well, as a former sheriff you should know it's against the law to ride around with someone who doesn't have a driver's license, let alone someone who is driving a toxic death wagon like this one." The policeman poked his head back into the car and spotted Puck.

"Who's the kid?"

"He's my grandson, and he's not feeling very well. We're taking him to a doctor," Granny said.

"Not in this thing, lady," the policeman said. "I'm impounding this vehicle for the good of humanity. I'll call an ambulance and have him taken to New York–Presbyterian Hospital."

He barked an order into his walkie-talkie as he eyed the family suspiciously.

"If Puck is sent to a hospital, they're going to discover he's not human," Sabrina mumbled to Granny Relda.

"The boy needs a special kind of doctor," Canis said to the cop.

"And the devil needs a glass of ice water," the officer snapped back. "You should be worrying about yourself. You're going to be lucky if you don't spend the night in jail. Do any of you have identification?"

"Of course," Granny Relda said as she reached into her handbag. "It's right here, somewhere."

But the police officer wasn't focused on the old woman. His eyes were glued on Mr. Canis and the big brown tail that had slipped out of the back of the old man's pants. The cop studied it for a moment, unsure of what it was, and then circled Mr. Canis to get a better look. Canis had suddenly grown several inches taller, and fangs were starting to pop out of his mouth.

"What's your story, buddy?" the policeman asked. "Are you going to a costume party or something?"

Canis's expression was nervous and angry. It was the same look he got when he struggled with his self-control.

"Stay calm," Sabrina whispered to Mr. Canis, but he didn't seem to hear her. A change was coming over him. His nose morphed into a hairy snout, and fur grew on his neck and hands. His body expanded, filling out the oversized suit he always wore. Black claws crept from the tips of his fingers. He was changing into the monster that lived inside him—the Big Bad Wolf.

The cop stood bewildered for a moment, then reached for his weapon.

"What are you?" he cried.

"Oh, here it is," Granny said as she pulled her hand from inside her purse, opened her fist, and blew a puff of pink dust into the cop's terrified face. He froze, and a look of befuddlement replaced his fear. His eyes went glassy, and his jaw went slack.

"You know, some days, being a policeman can be downright boring," Granny said as she placed a calming hand on the officer's shoulder.

"You're telling me," he said in a drowsy voice.

"Like today. Nothing interesting happened at all. You didn't even hand out a single speeding ticket."

"Yeah, today was real dull."

"Still, it was a nice enough day. In fact, you had a great afternoon out on patrol," Granny said.

"I did?" the officer said. "Yeah, I did."

"Thanks for your help, Officer, but we don't want to keep you any longer."

"I should be going," he said. Moments later, he hopped into his squad car and drove away.

"Lucky I brought the forgetful dust," Granny said. She rested the same calming hand on Mr. Canis's shoulder, and his savage transformation stopped, then slowly reversed, though the tail and enormous height didn't go away.

"Relda, I am sorry," he said. "Any little thing seems to set me off these days."

"No harm done," the old woman said. "But for the rest of this trip I suggest you hide your tail."

The old man nodded and did his best to tuck it into the back of his trousers.

"Wait a minute!" Sabrina exclaimed as she watched the squad car disappearing in the distance. On the back bumper, painted in bright white paint, were the letters NYPD. "That guy was a New York City cop!"

"Well, of course he was," Granny said as she pointed beyond the side of the bridge. Massive buildings reached skyward, as if competing for heaven's attention. Airplanes and helicopters flew above them.

Daphne squinted at the sparkling metropolis. One building stood taller than those around it, tapering at the top into a fine silver point. She grabbed her older sister's arm and pointed at it.

"That's the Empire State Building!" she cried, quickly placing the palm of her hand into her mouth and biting down on it. It was one of Daphne's many quirks—the one that signaled that she was happy and excited. "We're home!"

Sabrina's throat tightened as she fought back happy tears. "We're in New York City," she whispered.

ABOUT THE AUTHOR

Michael Buckley is the *New York Times* bestselling author of the Sisters Grimm and NERDS series, *Kel Gilligan's Daredevil Stunt Show*, and the Undertow Trilogy. He has also written and developed television shows for many networks. Michael lives in Brooklyn, New York, with his wife, Alison; their son, Finn; and their dog, Friday.